ANGEL MINE

Jimmy Taaffe

ARCHWAY
PUBLISHING

Archway Publishing books may be ordered through booksellers or by contacting:

Archway Publishing
1663 Liberty Drive
Bloomington, IN 47403
www.archwaypublishing.com
844-669-3957

ISBN: 978-1-6657-0825-8 (sc)
ISBN: 978-1-6657-0826-5 (e)

Library of Congress Control Number: 2021911989

Print information available on the last page.

Archway Publishing rev. date: 06/18/2021

The hardest thing in life is when the person who gave you the best memories becomes a memory.

PROLOGUE

Autumn quietly knocks like an expected, though not entirely unpleasant, guest. A light *tap tap tap* somewhere deep in your soul. Its pleasantness radiates into the room as you crack open the door just slightly to take a peek. You knew the kind old man was coming eventually, didn't you?

Weeks earlier, you sit on the back porch, a glass of wine in hand, watching the light slowly fade from the warm, late September sky. An almost sexual internal gush of anticipation floods your psyche. Indeed, change is coming. A change humans have felt for millions of years. You watch and wait for the leaves to ebb from green to brilliant reds and yellows. Even in the dog days, it's there, hidden just beneath the surface, ready to make its grand entrance. You breathe in deep and realize you can taste it. For the first time in months, you can feel the ever-so-slight chill in the fading light of a Sunday evening.

You close your eyes and walk slowly through the apple orchards, the crooked limbs reaching out to guide the way. The light is different somehow. Yellow and soft. The kind of natural light photographers love. You breathe. The rotting apples smell so tangy and sweet as the wind rustles the yellowing leaves. You stop in your tracks to take it all in. You breathe deeper. That tingle swirls up your spine. You know the one, don't you? The same tingle you got when you kissed a girl for the first time under the school bleachers so many years ago.

You look around as the grandness of life blankets you. You sit down between the endless rows of apple trees and pull your knees up tight to your chest to rest your chin. You listen as the bugs chirp and chime, like the world's smallest orchestra. Your tearful eyes gaze upward to a sky so blue that it's hard to imagine that soon the hand of God will slowly turn the grandest of the seasons into the darkest. Yet for now you breathe deep. Your change has come. Finally.

CHAPTER 1

Juju Apple blew her messy red hair away from her face with a quick puff of her breath while slamming down the turn signal.

"Fuck," she muttered to herself as she whipped her car onto Forbes Avenue and stomped on the gas pedal. Just as she turned the corner and began to accelerate, a Pittsburgh city bus slowly pulled out in front of her.

"Fuck!" she barked again in wide, blue-eyed disbelief. She shook her head in reserved dismay. The city bus puttered its exhaust at the windshield, like the fog of worry and doubt she had been living in for the last six months.

Sixth months ago, Juju's husband, Sidney, had taken the news of his pancreatic cancer with an attitude of mild contempt. But the cancer had spread like wildfire, and the doctor's optimistic outlook months ago faded into a distant memory. They sat in the oncologist's lavish office, and Juju glanced around the room with worry. She and Sid listened to the doctor spin confusing sentences they couldn't fully grasp. Something made her wonder whether these words were an intentionally clever design. As the doctor spoke, she reached out and held Sid's hand as the doctor went on with his seemingly rehearsed prognosis. At that moment she felt as if her world went askew, tipping over to the side.

Sidney turned and looked at her with slight defiance. "It's fine, Ju. It's going to be okay. You'll see."

Juju tried to keep her emotions in check for Sid's sake but failed and began to weep. Sid leaned over from his chair and held her. He whispered in her ear, "I'll fight this, baby. I'll beat it. I'll beat it." The battle lines had been drawn.

As soon as the opportunity presented itself, Juju mashed the accelerator and passed the city bus. "Jagoff," she muttered in a slight Pittsburgh-esque accent as she whizzed past the city bus and sped toward the hospital.

Juju whipped into the parking deck of the hospital and took the ticket from the machine. She stepped on the gas a little too early, and the roof of her car scraped the gate as it went up.

"Oh, for fuck's sake!" She scowled but didn't stop. She parked on the third level, got out, and opened the back hatch to grab her oversized bag full of necessities for the day. Three bottles of water, some magazines, a book about the stock market crash of 1929, a couple of Sid's favorite candy bars, and her ledger, which she had affectionately named Max.

The horn beeped twice in quick succession as she locked her car and walked briskly to the bank of elevators. She sighed, closing her eyes and breathing in deeply as she waited for the elevator, which would take her to the oncology wing and Sid's room. The doors opened, and Juju stepped inside, pressing the button for the eighth floor. Like a time machine, the elevator door swished shut.

As Juju was on her way up to the room, Joyce leaned against her son Sidney's bed. Her arms were crossed, with a constant look of irritation on her face. Just last week, she'd turned sixty-three, and now her great strides to look younger somehow made her look older. She rarely smiled and didn't give a damn what anyone thought. She wore her bitterness like some strange badge of honor.

Forty years ago, Joyce had been crowned Miss Pittsburgh at a lavish event at the Omni-Penn Hotel. Now, two husbands later, she looked tired and bitter. Sidney, her only child, was in the hospital bed in this damn hospital with this damn cancer, and her goddamn daughter-in-law was late.

Juju was well aware of Joyce's distaste for her. More than once she had seen that flash of resentment in Joyce's eyes. To the best of her knowledge, she had never been anything but kind and accommodating to her mother-in-law. Several times Ju had cornered Sid and demanded he explain his mother's actions.

"My mom is defective in some ways, Ju," he said. "She can be like the school bully on the playground. The bully leaves most people alone but will fixate on some people in particular. It's hard to say why, Ju—they just *do*."

Juju sniffed at this explanation and sighed. She often wondered how Sid's mother could have spawned such a loving and caring son. He was the polar opposite of his angry and damaged mother. Juju had never met her father-in-law, and Sid knew very little about the man other than he had been a firefighter from Philadelphia who had left Joyce shortly after she got pregnant. Juju suspected this rejection was the underlying cause of her mother-in-law's almost constant state of agitation, which seemed to embody her entire world and everyone who stepped into it.

Joyce glanced down at her watch again, then looked up sharply as Juju walked into the room.

Juju put her bags down and walked over to Sid's bedside. "Sorry, I'm a little bit behind. Traffic was bad. How is he?"

"No change," Joyce said curtly. "The doctor came by a little bit ago to check on him. I hoped you would be here."

Juju bit her lip and curled her toes at this passive-aggressive jab. She carefully leaned over and kissed Sid's forehead.

"You should have called me. I've been here for hours, and I'm tired," Joyce said.

Juju sighed and cocked her head. "You are not the only one running on fumes, Joyce. I just spent the last hour on the phone with the insurance company, and my patience is dwindling."

She took a small breath and against her better judgment let out a verbal punch. "Both you and the insurance company are on my very last nerve."

Joyce pursed her lips, preparing for the upcoming battle. "I'm going to let that slide, Ju," Joyce said. "I'm not sure how you can be so thoughtless sometimes."

Ju took a deep breath and turned toward her mother-in-law. "Joyce, you're right. I do tend to reflect my environment." She kissed Sidney's forehead again and started for the door.

"Where are you going?" Joyce snapped with authority.

"I'm going to the cafeteria to get Sid something to eat," she said firmly as she threw her oversized bag's strap over her shoulder.

Juju walked quickly out of the room toward the elevator, fists clenched. She pulled her journal, Max, from her bag, and quickly opened it, flipping pages to find the next blank page as she walked. Then she stopped in her tracks. "FUCK FUCK FUCK I LOVE HIM!" she wrote in big, bold letters. She snapped Max shut and put the ledger back into her bag. "Goddamnit!" she shouted in frustration, startling an elderly couple who stood by the elevator banks. Juju shot them an angry glare and marched quickly to the stairs. She threw the door open with a loud bang and ran down the five flights to the cafeteria to find fresh air.

CHAPTER 2

Jimmy Andrews focused on the paved bike trail in front of him, his body in perfect rhythm and timing. His breathing was heavy but smooth. His face, tanned from his daily bike rides, had a wisp of a smile on it. He rounded the trail and caught up to the big freight train lumbering down the tracks, which ran parallel to the bike trail. His feet pedaled smoothly as he raced side by side with the train but only briefly. The train soon gained speed and left Jimmy pedaling behind it.

Moments later he scooted off the trail and onto the paved city streets of Struthers, Ohio. A small town with a handful of traffic lights, it was located an hour north of Pittsburgh and an hour south of Cleveland. He looked down at his iPhone and was pleased with his twenty-five-mile ride. He cooled down as he slowly pedaled his bike to his parked car by the railroad tracks a quarter mile away. The tail end of the train was just passing as he arrived at his car. He popped the tailgate of his SUV open and rested his trusty bike inside.

It was the height of summer, with the world so green and lush that it made him dizzy to look at it. A fine time for kids, children who played in the park, their thoughts of school still so far away. It was a happy time for all, including Jimmy, and why shouldn't it be? Jimmy and his beautiful wife, Kristy, had a wonderful home and great careers. At forty-six years old, he felt as though he were at the peak of his life. He thought of all the wonderful things he was blessed with, most of all for being in love with Kristy.

Jimmy sat behind the wheel of his SUV for a moment, watching as two young boys, with fishing poles thrown over their shoulders like carbines, made their way down to the Mahoning River. Probably to spend the day with their feet in the river, hoping for a good catch. He toweled off his face and the back of his neck, then quickly took a drink from his water bottle. He sighed a contented breath and turned over the engine to head home, remembering Kristy had said she would be there for lunch.

Jimmy's daily routine included a bike ride and yoga. His job as a photographer afforded him the luxury of living his life on his own schedule. After twelve years in his profession, he was now an award-winning, international photographer. This was a title that made him smile with just a smidge of vain satisfaction. Saturdays, of course, were reserved for weddings, but the rest of the week was his to make his own. His faithful bride, Kristy, was also a photographer. Yet unlike Jimmy, she specialized in photographing children. This was a skill Jimmy had never quite been able to grasp. Kids loved her. Everyone loved her. She was the ultimate woman. They had an amazing and somewhat simple life, and Jimmy felt blessed that she loved their life too. She added the splashes of color to their world.

Jimmy slowed his car to cross the railroad tracks on Poland Avenue and continued home. He looked at the clock and knew Kristy might be waiting for him to eat. He turned the radio up and tapped his fingers on the wheel as Rush started singing about being in the "Limelight."

CHAPTER 3

Kristy and her best friend, Shannon Raptis, couldn't stop laughing. Their friendship was relatively new but had grown amazingly strong in a short time. Two years earlier, Kristy had seen Shannon at the jogging trail down the street from her house almost every day. Finally, with a deep breath, Kristy had struck up a conversation with her, and the two clicked like girls do. It wasn't long before they were inseparable. Jogging, spinning, and chatting almost daily over coffee.

The pair of besties pedaled side by side in spinning class, glancing occasionally at each other and giggling. Their laughter wasn't directed at anything specific; it was just goofy, contagious laughter, and they couldn't stop. Like at church. The church of spinning and body sculpting.

Kristy and Shannon agreed that they were "laughaholics." More than once, the spinning instructor shot them a disapproving look, like a nun in spandex. Those looks made them snicker even more, despite the icy glances from the debutantes in the class, who all looked like the instructor.

After class finished and they were toweling off in the locker room, Shannon asked Kristy, "Should we grab a cup of coffee. Or maybe an early lunch?"

"No, honey, I can't today. I am going to surprise Jimmy with a wifey lunch," Kristy said, cocking her eyebrow.

"Oh, is that what they call it these days?" Shannon said, smiling. "I can't remember the last time I had a *wifey* lunch with Pete. He's always so busy with work."

"Oh. nothing fancy. It's just fun to make time for those romantic surprises. Keeps the love alive," Kristy said, lacing up her shoes.

Both girls grabbed their bags and high-stepped out of the locker room to the lobby and out the large glass front doors. "See you back here tomorrow?" Shannon asked.

Kristy said, "No, sweetheart. They're closed for the Fourth of July holiday!"

They giggled and said, "Duh" simultaneously, gave each other a quick hug and kiss on the cheek goodbye, then trotted off to their cars. Kristy pulled out first and gave Shannon a quick wave. Shannon beeped twice and left in the opposite direction.

As Kristy made her way down the road, she felt a slight yet alarming twinge in her chest. The stabbing pain lasted only a moment or two. "The fuck?" she mumbled, rubbing her chest bone, puzzled. Her first thought was that she'd somehow pulled a muscle in her chest. Or maybe it was heartburn. Either way, she didn't dwell on it. The pain faded just as quickly as it had occurred; otherwise, she felt just fine.

The rest of the drive home was uneventful, except for the traffic that slowed her almost to a halt. She sang along with Tom Petty about being an "American Girl," not letting the traffic hamper her otherwise-fine mood. Tapping her fingers on the steering wheel to the beat, she ran through a mental list of errands to run later that afternoon. The bank. Oil change for her car. Maybe the post office for Fourth of July American flag stamps. Perhaps she'd swing by her mom's for a coffee and chitchat. It had been a week since she'd seen her mom, and Kristy had no doubt there would be plenty of family dish to catch up on.

Twenty minutes later, she pulled into her driveway and saw Jimmy's car wasn't there, which meant he was still on his morning bicycle ride. She smiled, knowing she had some time to plan. Even after years of marriage, little romantic things still excited her. They were both still very much in love and smitten.

Kristy jumped out of the car and waved to their neighbor, Evie, who was getting ready to mow the lawn. The sun was shining brightly, and it was turning out to be a beautiful day.

CHAPTER 4

With a swoosh of sunlight behind her, Juju's mom, Cathy, whom everyone called "Cookie," sped out of the Fort Pitt tunnel into downtown Pittsburgh. As she took the Bigelow Boulevard exit, she held onto the Crock-Pot of soup with one hand and negotiated the turn with the other. The hospital was just five quick blocks away.

As usual, she was early. A habit she'd picked up from her father, she supposed. He was fond of saying, "If you are on time, you are already late." He was famous for countless life sayings one should live by. And even after all these years, Cookie remembered almost all of them.

In an almost comical comparison, Cookie was the complete opposite of Joyce, her daughter's mother-in-law. Like her daughter, Ju, Cookie was a free spirit and loved everything about life. Even with her wonderful son-in-law, Sid, in the hospital with cancer, Cookie outwardly remained strong and optimistic despite her silent concern, constantly comforting her daughter and peppering positive remarks to her.

Cookie rehearsed in her mind more than once how she was going to handle Ju when Sid inevitably passed away. Her husband had died when Ju was in high school, and her heart ached for what Ju was going to experience in the coming months. She knew all too well what was on the horizon for her only daughter. She remembered with painful and vivid color her experience many years ago of climbing down into that rabbit hole, that surreal and frightening place no person should see. One thing she was sure of: she was going stand by Ju as much as she could.

Just as Cookie pulled into the hospital parking deck, her cell phone rang. A glance at the ID, and she saw it was Ju. "Hi baby, I'm just pulling into the deck," she said while craning her neck to find a parking space.

"Hi, Mom," Ju said. "Did you bring soup?"

Cookie switched ears and pulled carefully into a spot close to the elevators. "Yeah, baby, I did. I'll be up in a minute. Is Joyce still here?" She cringed as she waited for Ju to answer. Unlike her daughter, Cookie simply smiled and placated Joyce with gentle nods and smiles. But privately her aversion for the way Joyce treated not only her daughter but generally every person who crossed her path was palpable.

"She just left. Don't be surprised if you pass her in the hall on the way in," Ju said blankly.

Cookie debated just sitting in her car for a few minutes to give Joyce time to leave but quickly decided not to. "Well, I'm coming up, and if I run into her, I run into her. Is bitchiness contagious?"

This out-of-character remark made Juju spontaneously giggle. "Mom!" she whispered hoarsely with shock. They both laughed aloud.

"Well, I'm sorry Ju. But she's a viper."

Juju shrieked with laughter. "Maaaaaom!" Ju covered her mouth, and from between her fingers, she said, "Mom, I love you. I'll see you in a few."

Cookie smiled and hung up.

Ju drew a deep breath and ducked into the bathroom to pee. Moments later, washing her hands, she spent a second to look at herself in the mirror. She brushed her sloppy red hair away from her face and exhaled sharply. She ignored the red circles under her eyes and flipped the light off with a firm snap.

Ju sat down next to Sid and waited for her mom. She took a long look at her husband and started to cry. She wept silently, her hands covering her face. A minute later Cookie walked in, put her Crock-Pot down, and rushed to Juju.

"Honey, I'm here," Cookie said. She held her daughter tight and helped her cry. Two generations of women, wrapped together by a common thread of losing someone they loved way too soon. They wept silently in each other's arms.

CHAPTER 5

Kristy showered quickly and dressed. She figured Jimmy was probably finished racing trains on his bike and should be home shortly. She pulled on black yoga pants and a thin white T-shirt, then ran out front to get the mail. It had gotten even warmer outside since she got home.

She raised an eyebrow when she saw a package addressed for Jimmy among the bundle of bills and junk mail. She came inside, sorted the mail, and looked at the package, deciding to open it. It was a new Pittsburgh Pirates jersey. Of course, it was! After all, Jimmy had an entire closet full of Pittsburgh Pirates jerseys. She smiled, thinking, *What's one more?*

This gave her an idea.

Ah, yes, this will be a surprise he will not soon forget!

She took off her white T-shirt and put on the jersey. Walking into the bedroom quickly, she looked at herself in the full-length mirror. "Hubba-hubba," she whispered, pushing out her ample breasts. She turned from side to side to see how she looked in the jersey. She thought how sexy she looked with the button open and her favorite black bra showing.

Kristy looked at the clock; it was almost noon. Almost time for lunch. Bustling around the kitchen, looking for something quick to make for Jimmy, she pulled out the bread and peanut butter. No jelly. *Okay.*

So instead she went to the take-out menu drawer. She barely noticed the quick, little flutter of discomfort in her chest as she leaned against the kitchen counter, going through the menus.

She decided on pizza. Pizza and Pirates. Yes, Jimmy's dream. And with that thought, she heard him pull in the driveway. Taffy, their loyal greyhound, jumped up and went to the door to greet Jimmy.

"Hi, baby. I'm home!" Jimmy called out as he swung the door open and kicked off his biking shoes. "Taffy! Are you a good girl?" Jimmy said as Taffy wagged away affirmatively. He gave their beloved dog a little scratch on her head.

Kristy called from the kitchen, "Are you hungry, baby?"

"Yeah, I'll eat," he replied as he walked into the kitchen with Taffy in tow.

Kristy was leaning on the counter, holding up the menus. Jimmy instead noticed the partly open Pirates jersey. He smiled and without a word gave Kristy a long kiss, pulling her in close.

"So you *are* hungry," Kristy cooed, showing him the empty jelly jar.

Jimmy ginned. "Peanut butter and Pittsburgh Pirates sandwiches, it is!"

They ate a quiet lunch on the back patio. They chatted about the weddings they had coming up that they needed to photograph, then talked about going to the Outer Banks this fall. Kristy loved going there. She looked forward to the trip down to the Carolinas every year.

They finished eating, and Kristy walked over to the doorway of the porch, leaning on the frame. She said, "A little pregame?"

Jimmy looked up, smiling, and followed her to the bedroom. Kristy threw her cell phone on the end of the bed and leaned seductively over Jimmy, exposing her bra as she stretched out on the bed. She whispered in his ear, "Wanna fuck?"

Jimmy grinned and smacked her butt as she lay across his lap. "Sure do!"

Kristy laughed her soft laugh.

CHAPTER 6

Juju sat in the corner chair of Sid's hospital room, reading her book about early art history and its influence on modern culture. The afternoon had just started, and outside, the sun blazed hot over Pittsburgh. The television was on with the volume turned off. Occasionally, Juju glanced up and take note of the Pirates pregame.

Juju and Sid were finally alone. Cookie had left, and the endless parade of friends and family had finally paused. Juju saw this as a great relief, since the last small group said their goodbyes and promised to be back tomorrow. Her eyes raised slightly over her retro-pink reading glasses as Sid stirred and turned toward her. His voice was raspy, his thin face gaunt and spent.

"Hey Ju," he said quietly.

"Hey, baby." Ju leaned in, closing her book softly. Her face smiled sadly.

Sid was struggling to talk. "Do you remember the time we sat on those swings? The ones on top of Mount Washington? The ones with the view of the city? I think it was maybe our second date."

Juju nodded. Her eyes were already filling with tears.

Sid pushed on with a weak smile and said, "That was a good time, Ju. Don't forget that time, okay? … Ever."

Juju nodded quickly. Sid lay on his back and closed his eyes. His breathing became steady yet labored.

Her mind shifted and flashed back to that summer evening on Mount Washington so many years ago. She had sat on the swing while Sid pushed her higher and higher. Her distinct contagious laugh had echoed through the trees and across the playground. Her red hair swept back from her face, and her eyes closed as Sid pushed her higher and higher. She giggled like she was a little girl again.

As they played on the swing, the city began to light up below them. They stopped to sit side by side and held hands, looking at Pittsburgh spread out from high above. Juju listened to Sid talk, and for the first time in her life, the phrase "drunk love" came into her head. *Yep, he is the one*, she thought. They both smiled, rocking back and forth on those swings, watching the lights of the big buildings flicker on and chatting about all things, both great and small. No, she would never forget. Ever.

Sid fell asleep, so Ju went to the cafeteria to get lunch and bring it back to the room. As she dined on the mediocre hospital food, she put her big art history book on the floor and picked up her ledger, Max, slowly flipping through the pages. The weight of her old ledger felt comforting sitting on her lap. This was the same ledger she had been writing her thoughts in for as long as she could remember. Its olive-green cover was marbled and aged. The pages in between had been replaced thousands of times. Each time the stack of pages was completely filled with words, she would oh so carefully pull them out and replace them with fresh, clean paper. Then, as carefully as she could, she took them to her filing cabinet and gently placed them in a folder, marked with the starting date and finishing date. Some folders were thick and bursting with thoughts and emotions, while some lay thin and almost empty. This was her lifeboat, her escape from what she thought might do her harm.

Sometimes Juju wrote feverishly and with adolescent hyperactivity, while other times her pen dripped with elegant script and poise. No matter which way her mood swung her, this was her escape hatch. In a weird way Max was her best friend. As a teenager, she spent hours with this ledger across her lap, writing airy poetry and sketching pictures of people she had seen on the streets of Pittsburgh. When she was an adult, her writing took on a darker, more cynical mood. Sometimes when she finished writing out her emotions, she closed the ledger with a snap, angrily biting her bottom lip. It was her way of exorcising those demons.

Her dad had gotten her the ledger as a gift when she turned twelve. On her birthday, a rainy and chilly April Saturday, he had sat her down on his workbench in the basement. The gift was wrapped in newspaper with a bright-pink bow attached. She reached out and took it with careful gentleness. She slowly unwrapped it and stared at this oversized green ledger. Her dad began to speak as his calloused hands lifted her chin to look at him.

"Jujubear … you have talent, baby. A talent most people can only dream about. Your heart—it's so pure."

He was leaning against the workbench as he spoke. The single light bulb cast a dim glow in his small corner room, which was tucked away in the basement of their house. This was the place where her dad came to tinker with little things and make his homemade fishing lures. Juju always thought of it as a place of great happiness and joy. She would sit for hours with her dad and watch him fix lamps and build little railroad cars for his model railroad town, which he had meticulously set up in the room next to his workshop. They talked for hours about trains, baseball, boys, and silly things daddies and daughters talked about. He taught her so many things as he sat on his chair and fiddled with whatever project he happened to be working on at the time.

"Jujubear, this world … it's a wonderful place. It's a beautiful place. Try not to forget that. Your entire life, people are going to tell you how the world's no damn good and people are no damn good. Don't listen to them, Ju. The world *is* good, and so are people. God gave you this talent to draw and see things in a light not too many people do. And it's your job to never let people forget how breathtaking this world is. Do you understand, Ju?"

She nodded. Even at the tender age of twelve, she understood completely. "Daddy, I need a special pen to write and draw with."

"Ahhhh … so you do!" her father said loudly and walked over to the furnace. Behind it he had an antique quill pen and a small bottle of ink on the shelf. He carefully pulled them off and walked back to his workbench. He handed the pen and inkwell to his daughter, and with her big-blue eyes and sloppy red hair, she gazed up at him.

"This is a quill pen, honey. You dip the tip into this ink and write. You have to dip the pen back in the ink as soon as the ink on the paper gets lighter. You'll get the hang of it, Ju. It's kind of a lost art."

Juju smiled and examined the pen and ink very closely. She stopped and looked up at her daddy with her big blue eyes. "Thank you, Daddy. I love it. I love you."

Her dad smiled and hugged her tight. "Go get washed up for dinner, baby."

Juju obediently ran up the stairs from the basement to her room and shut the door. She jumped on her bed and sat cross-legged; she carefully twisted the cap and opened the little bottle of ink. She slowly opened her new ledger and looked down at the blank page. In her mind's eye, she was instantly able to turn the blank page into a collage of words, pictures, and images, which was something she had always been able to do. She could stand in front of a blank wall as color and words dripped and cascaded down, instantly filling the blank void in her mind's eye. By the time she was six or seven, she was able to hold a brush or pen to fill the lines and turn the empty space into a world of amazing color.

She gave herself a brief second; then oh so carefully, she dipped the pen in the ink. When the pen touched paper, she wrote to herself, "Hello, new friend! My name is Juju Apple. Can I call you Max?" From there a lifetime bond had been formed between Ju and Max. A bond that would get her through the toughest times of her life and of course the absolute best of times.

Now today, so many years later, Ju picked up Max and slowly opened the cover. She looked around the sterile hospital room, then down at the blank page and began to write. "Hello, Max, I am so afraid."

CHAPTER 7

Jimmy and Kristy sat on their big bed and flipped through the channels, looking for the next best thing to watch. A quick minute later, Kristy said rather plainly and without any alarm in her voice, "Baby, I don't feel good."

Jimmy felt her arms wrap around him, slightly tight. He looked over at the clock and looked back, starting to say something. Her eyes were now closed as her grip on him relaxed.

Jimmy immediately knew something was dreadfully wrong. He thought at first maybe she had fainted, but instinctively and quickly he realized she hadn't. With an unmatched degree of urgency, every alarm in his body went off simultaneously. He called her name. No response. Again, he called her name. Nothing.

The panic quickly swelled, and he shook her and held her face in both of his hands. "Kristy! … Kristy! Oh God, Kristy!" She wasn't breathing.

He leaned over her and grabbed her phone to dial 9-1-1. He told the dispatcher to send an ambulance right away, that his wife wasn't breathing. Screaming in a deliberately articulate voice, he said to her, "I called 9-1-1. Just hang on, baby. Just hang on!"

Sensing something was wrong, Taffy started to bark and pace by the bedroom door as Jimmy started CPR on Kristy.

How much time had passed now? He didn't know. He was fighting to keep his wife alive. Crying as he performed CPR, he kept mumbling under his breath, "I love you, baby. Hang on. Hang on. Hang on."

After what seemed like a lifetime, he felt someone pulling on him and realized it was the paramedics from the Struthers Fire Department. Jimmy hadn't heard them come in the front door.

"We got her … we got her," the paramedic said sternly while pulling Jimmy off.

He stumbled backward a little, and his back hit the wall. He watched them put the blood pressure cuff on and listen to her heart. He was having a hard time understanding what was happening as if he had instantly been dropped into some type of vivid and horrible dream. The entire room seemed to be in an old kaleidoscope. The paramedics were frantically working on her. Jimmy's ears began to buzz, and things started to get very gray around the edges.

A quick moment later someone was pulling him gently yet firmly out of the room. It was a Struthers police officer.

"Come on. They got her. They got her. Let's give them some room," the officer said calmly while trying to use his knee to get Taffy out of the way. He led Jimmy down the hall and out to the front porch.

The policeman went back into the house just as the ambulance pulled up. Two more paramedics ran across the front yard and into the house, pushing past Jimmy without saying a word. Jimmy walked out onto the driveway and stood there alone, arms hanging by his sides. A moment later, one of the paramedics burst out of the front door, ran across the yard to the ambulance, and grabbed a bag from the back of the ambulance. He ran back in the house.

Jimmy stood there, watching in complete disbelief. *Why is he running so fast?* he numbly thought.

Jimmy rode with her to the hospital in the ambulance. On the way, he made the necessary phone calls to Kristy's mom, Lauren; her dad, Ray; and his parents. He tried his best to keep his composure, but he was quickly falling apart, and he sensed that the paramedics in the back knew something was very wrong.

Family arrived at the hospital, while the doctors worked in vain to revive Kristy. The minutes ticked by, and Jimmy came to the unimaginable realization that she may not live. He was able to go between the private waiting area and the small emergency room where Kristy was. She was surrounded by a group of ten doctors and nurses, who were all working on her feverishly. He noticed one very young doctor, probably a medical student, standing back and observing but ready to jump in, if needed. They made eye contact for a very brief second, and the young doctor's face said it all. It was at that point that Jimmy knew.

He knew.

She was going to die.

The lead doctor, a gray-haired man with wire-rim glasses, called the family into the room to tell them the unimaginable news. Kristy's mom, Lauren, wept into her hands, and her father stood next to her, stone faced and pale. Jimmy had to lean against the doorjamb to keep his balance.

There was only so much that could be done. The pain in her chest she had been feeling throughout the day had been more serious than she thought.

Months later, Jimmy sat at the kitchen table, reading the autopsy report, which indicated that she had suffered from a rare heart disease called ARVD. He drew a deep breath, folded the report in half, and cried into his hands for a long time.

In the blink of an eye, Jimmy's world had crashed around him. He swallowed hard and walked over to Kristy, who lay on the hospital gurney. He laid his head on her chest and cried as the doctors, nurses, and her parents stood silently around him. They all seemed to be looking down at their feet, not wanting to witness the grief, as they silently brushed the tears away.

She was gone. The absolute love of Jimmy's life was gone.

CHAPTER 8

The sun would soon start to set, making the sky explode with brilliant reds and oranges, as Juju sat quietly on the windowsill. Her glazed and red-rimmed eyes scanned the city of Pittsburgh as the cascade of colors in the sky unfolded in front of her. The room was eerily quiet except for the steady and comforting sounds of Sidney's breathing and the distant chatter from the nurses at their station at the end of the hall. The room was lit by a single small lamp next to the bed.

Occasionally turning away from the city and sky, she looked at Sydney's face and smiled sadly, then returned to looking out the window high above the city below. She felt completely helpless and useless. A feeling she wasn't used to. A feeling that felt completely alien to her.

She knew the end was coming despite the doctor's robotic optimism and artificial cheer. The doctor gave her and the family large amounts of complicated information, which seemed to be designed to keep them placated. Most of the time as he spoke, Juju found herself drifting in and out of her haze. Despite all the bullshit the doctor was telling her, one thing was for sure: Sid was going to die. It occurred to Juju that the doctor felt as useless as she did.

She stood up and walked over to Sid's side; she pulled the small stool over and sat down quietly. She reached out to touch his face; then she took his hand gingerly and squeezed it. The soft light flickered on her face. Her normally bright eyes were drained and wrinkled with stress and grief.

She had always been a strangely attractive girl. The kind of girl whose beauty others couldn't quite put your finger on, the girl Sidney had once called "his strange savage and great beauty." She was the kind of girl others may or may not notice in a crowd. If they did notice her, they would raise their eyebrows slightly when they looked at her, intrigued by her angelic beauty.

"Love, don't go away," she said with a choked and heavy whisper. She slowly shook her head. "Don't go. Don't leave, love."

Sidney died forty-five minutes later. One last time, his chest rose and held itself, then fell, never to rise again. Juju let out a small, harsh gasp and began to cry. "Oh, Sidney." she cried softly with her head on his chest. "Oh, my love," she whispered.

A long minute later, quivering, she reached over and rang for the nurse to come.

CHAPTER 9

Jimmy had no idea how he got home from the hospital that evening after leaving Kristy. He felt as if he had a constant case of extreme vertigo, and flashes in time were all he could deal with right now. The house was filling up with family and friends, but he couldn't hear what people were saying. It was just garbled white noise to him. People's lips were moving, but nothing was registering to him. More than once, a gray fog filled his mind, and he began to feel weak and faint. Eventually, he found his way into the bathroom at the end of the hall and went in. With the door locked, he sat on the floor and began to cry. He pulled his knees to his chest and closed his eyes tight as the tears flowed easily.

Jimmy moved only when he heard Taffy pawing at the door. He crawled over, reached up, and unlocked the door. From his knees, he turned the knob, and Taffy rushed in. "Good girl," Jimmy choked out as he wrapped his arms around the hound and squeezed. "You're a good girl." Taffy wagged her tail in agreement as they both leaned against the toilet while Jimmy tried to get his bearings. After fifteen minutes, Jimmy and Taffy came out of the bathroom and into the kitchen. The house was filled with people, many Jimmy wasn't sure he even knew.

Kristy's mom, Lauren, immediately came over to Jimmy with her eyes rimmed red from crying. She was constantly wringing her hands.

"Are you okay?" Lauren asked in a low voice.

"No," he said simply, went into his bedroom, locked the door, and laid his face down on the bed, where only hours earlier, Kristy had died. He breathed deeply into her pillow and began to cry.

CHAPTER 10

Juju wasn't sure how she had gotten to the top of Mount Washington and over to West End Park that day. Months later this would perplex her, and with mild wonder, she thought about this over and over. The last thing she remembered was leaving the hospital after Sid died. She vaguely remembered ringing for the nurse and kissing Sid's forehead before she walked out of his room and ran down the hall, crying and sobbing. She didn't remember anything about the twenty-minute drive from the hospital to the park on Mount Washington. Her memory cleared and came into soft focus as she remembered sitting on the swing, the same one she and Sid had sat on during their second date years ago. It was as if she had brushed away the fog of pain just long enough for her to look around and see where she was and what she could expect.

Now she sat on that swing alone.

After their second date, Ju and Sid had come here often, looking out over the city of Pittsburgh and talking about the future and the wonderful life they were going to have. She'd run her fingers through his hair as they sat looking out at the skyline. They talked, laughed, and dreamed of all manner of things. It was always very clear to Juju how lucky she was to have him and how lucky she was to have a life like this. It was the life she had always dreamed of. A life with him.

The wind picked up slightly, and Juju could see the heat lightning pounding the north hills in the distance. She sat still and quiet in her solitude. The row of streetlights lining the walkway to the parking lot flickered, while somewhere in the distance she could hear children laughing.

She couldn't move. She could feel that her blank, tear-stained face was frozen in a look of absolute heartbreak. Occasionally, a light gust of wind blew her red hair away from her face, revealing her obvious pain in strange technicolor. She was mildly aware of the almost-constant buzzing of her cell phone in her pocket. She knew her house would be filling up, and her family would be very worried about her. She looked up into the early evening sky, took a long glance at the low-flying jet headed into Pittsburgh International Airport, and sighed deeply.

"Time and tide," she whispered as she stood up slowly.

Juju walked the curved sidewalk back to her car, crying silently. The car door popped open, and Ju slid in. Moments later she was speeding across the Mount Washington neighborhood on her way home. She never stopped crying.

CHAPTER 11

At midnight on the Fourth of July, the day after Kristy died, Jimmy was alone in bed with her side untouched and neatly made. The neighborhood fireworks were now coming to an end. The moonlight spilled across the floor in strange, wispy patterns, while a soft wind from the open window gently blew the curtains in slow, methodical circles, like dancers in some fantastic ballet.

Lying on his back with his hands folded neatly on his chest, Jimmy whispered, "Kristy." He held his breath as the moment spun out.

Again, "Kristy."

Nothing.

In some ethereal way, he almost expected some type of response.

Somewhere in the dark corners of his mind, certain realizations began to take hold. He was alone. She used to tease him that he would make an excellent bachelor, and most of the time he didn't argue; he simply shrugged, and she smiled.

But now, what was he going to do? He knew the worst was yet to come. He knew that soon enough the numbness was going to fade away, and the pain was going to latch on to him and not let go. He reluctantly started to let his mind wander and drift in the darkness of his bedroom. Half of him was gone now, and he wondered to himself, *How could this be happening?* Was he just dreaming? No, he wasn't dreaming. This was real, and no amount of praying and pleading was going to change that.

The thoughts started flooding on him like a harsh, cold rain. What on earth was he going to do? How was he going to survive without her? The tears flowed. He leaned over, put his face into her pillow, and cried. As he silently wept, he could smell her on the pillow, which only made him cry harder.

The night pressed endlessly on and on, and when sleep finally came, it was broken, choppy, and dreamless. More than once, he reached over to her side of the bed, hoping to feel her soft skin.

Just before dawn, he rolled out of bed and looked out the back bedroom window. The sun was just starting to rise, cutting the trees in the woods into slices of shadows.

"Another day," he whispered to himself.

The back lawn was sprinkled with a million dewy, little diamonds. With childlike wonder he wished he could scoop them up by the handful and ransom his life back.

Jimmy sighed, stretched, opened his mental notebook, and started going through his day. He felt achy and sad, and he wasn't looking forward to the laundry list of errands he needed to run. Kristy's sister Linda had come into town late last night from Washington, DC. She'd pulled into Jimmy's driveway just before midnight, and they'd spent only a short time talking before they both went to sleep for the night. He felt a little relief, knowing he could count on her to help out with the details. With a heavy, deep breath, he walked out to the kitchen and started the coffee maker. This was the first day of the rest of his life without her.

Later that morning, Jimmy and Linda began the laborious task of planning Kristy's funeral. Linda seemed as if she constantly needed to catch her breath and had a handful of tissues with her at all times.

The first of many stops was to the funeral home on Poland Avenue. Kristy's father, Ray, had gone to school with the owner and recommended using the well-established home. On the way over to the funeral home, Jimmy stared out the window as Linda drove.

"I didn't sleep very well last night. In a weird kind of way … I don't know … I'm afraid," Jimmy said as they sped down the road.

The car turned onto Poland Avenue, and Jimmy continued, "I keep thinking about who's going to take care of the little things. Who am I going to talk to? Who's going to scratch my back? Who's going to get me through the tough times?"

He drew a deep breath, and his eyes began to fill with tears for the hundredth time that day. "God, I miss her so much already. How much am I going to miss her next week? Next month? Next year? Is this going to get any better?"

Linda was now crying too. She had her pain to deal with, and she vaguely wondered whether Jimmy understood that. Then she thought, *Do I fully understand his?*

"Jimmy, she loved you so much," Linda said as she pulled into the funeral home. She turned off the motor.

"She loved you too," Jimmy said, trying to blink the tears out of his eyes.

They looked at one another for a long moment, then opened the doors and stepped out of the car.

The funeral home staff welcomed them as they stepped out of the heat and into the air-conditioned lobby.

"Hello, Mr. Andrews. Hello, Miss Wolfe," the planning coordinator said with a soft, well-rehearsed voice. "Let me start by extending our deepest sympathies to you and your family."

"Thank you, we appreciate that," Linda said as Jimmy looked around nervously.

The funeral director, Mrs. Kane, led them to a private office. Jimmy and Linda sat down and started the painful task of picking out a casket and exploring all the other countless details. Jimmy took most of the recommendations Mrs. Kane put forth without much input. He let Linda do most of the talking as he stared down at his feet. When asked a question, he answered quietly but really just wanted to go home. He wanted to wake up from this nightmare, from this very vivid dream he *must* be having.

This can't be real, can it?

A few days later, hundreds upon hundreds of family and friends showed up at the funeral to pay their respects. Throughout the entire day, Jimmy felt as if his world were somehow inverted; this vivid dream just continued hour by hour. He was having a difficult time understanding what people were saying to him. It was as if they were speaking in some strange tongue. A great many of the mourners all seemed to be reading from the same scripted page. He just politely smiled and thanked them for coming. At times he felt like an actor in a poorly written play.

By the time Jimmy got home that night, he was mentally exhausted. Both Linda and Kristy's mom, Lauren, were staying at the house, and as Jimmy sat slumped on the couch, he could hear both women bustling in the kitchen.

"Do you want some soup or a sandwich?" Linda said, peeking around the corner.

Jimmy shrugged. "Sure, thanks."

Linda smiled lightly and disappeared back into the kitchen. The sound of the dishes being stacked and the food being made seemed almost deafening to him. It felt as if the volume in his head was suddenly turned up to ten. Jimmy took a deep breath, sat up, and walked into his bedroom. Inadvertently, he slammed the bedroom door harder than he thought he did.

In the kitchen, Linda and Lauren looked at each other, concerned, with brows raised.

CHAPTER 12

Juju spent the morning of Sidney's funeral in a blank far-off place in her mind. Her mom, Cookie, was at arm's length the entire morning, hovering close to her broken-hearted daughter. Cookie, who had lost her husband, Ben, some twenty years ago, still remembered the pain of losing a spouse and being a young widow.

Juju's dad had died when she was seventeen, leaving Cookie a widow with two children, Juju and her brother, Matt, who had been twenty-six at the time. Cookie never remarried or even dated for that matter. After Ben died, Cookie made the conscious decision not to date or even to expand her social circle.

"Ju, do you need anything?" Cookie asked softly. Juju didn't answer. She stood with her back to her mom, looking in her oversized closet. Cookie stood in the bedroom doorway with her arms crossed tightly across her chest. "Honey, I'm here for you."

Juju turned around to face her mom. Her shoulders slumped. She stood there with her head down and started to sob hysterically. Cookie rushed to her daughter and held her, "Shhhhh ... Ju, I'm here. Mom's here."

She held her daughter in much the same way her mom, Rose, had held her some twenty years before when Cookie was going through the same thing. "I'm here, Juju. I'm here."

Cookie held her daughter and stroked her hair as she sobbed and cried on her shoulder. Cookie's tears fell down her cheeks onto Juju's hair. Cookie said quietly, "Come on, baby. Let's find something for you to wear today."

Juju nodded and took deep breaths to try to get her crying under control. They found a black dress that met both of their high standards, and Juju laid it out on the bed.

"Mom, I'm not sure I can do this," she said through the sobs. "I don't know if I can face all the people. Mom, I don't want to go." She started crying again.

"I know, Ju. I know." Cookie softly rubbed her back. They both sat down on the corner of the bed. "Ju, look at me, honey. This is going to be the hardest thing you will ever have to do and something you shouldn't have to do. It's not fair, yet let's push through it together." They looked at each other and leaned forward, touching foreheads.

An hour later, Juju, her mom, her brother, Matt, and her best friend, Cheryl, all drove out to the funeral home. The ride was somber. Juju held her mom's hand the entire time. Matt drove, and he looked sad and defeated. Cheryl, breaking the silence, made some light chat about the weather and traffic. As they pulled into the funeral home, Juju was surprised to see a huge amount of cars and people already there. Calling hours weren't scheduled to start for another hour.

As the rest of the family began to fill the funeral home in Greentree, a steady, light rain began to fall, dampening the mood even more. Juju was able to sit with Sidney alone for a few minutes before the calling hours were set to begin. She spoke quietly to him, most of the time just above a whisper. She told him how much she loved him and how much she was going to miss him. She sat in a small chair and leaned against the coffin, while her tears silently flowed down her cheeks. Just as she was getting up, Matt slowly opened the sliding door to the viewing room, and asked, "Ju, you need anything?"

She shook her head and stood up. "Wait, Matt. Can you get me something to drink? A bottle of water or something?"

Matt nodded and quickly ducked out into the hall. He looked over his shoulder at his little sister and held back his tears.

Ju turned to Sidney. "Goodbye, my sweet love." She leaned over him and kissed him one last time.

Cookie and Sidney's mother, Joyce, stood with Juju as the lines of mourners and family slowly made their way past the casket and gave their condolences to Ju and the mothers. Ju kept looking over to Sidney, heartbroken. More than once, she reached down and pinched her leg in a childish gesture that she might wake up and this nightmare would be over. Outside, the drizzle turned into a storm, and the muffled sounds of thunder filled the room.

Two weeks later, Juju parked her car at the top of the hill at Allegheny Cemetery under a big oak tree and turned the motor off. She sat in her parked car for a minute, trying to catch her breath, then opened the door and slowly stepped out. She drew one last deep breath and began to walk the cemetery path to where Sidney had been laid to rest; she looked around, feeling a little distant. The elms and maples hung over the path in a Norman Rockwell-esque scene as the gentle July wind blew, light, steady, and warm across her face.

Under any other circumstances, she would have noticed the wonderful, strange beauty of this place, but today she didn't. This was now a place that drained her strength. A place that made her feel like her soul had been abandoned from its rightful place and somehow vanished from existence, maybe or maybe not to be seen again.

She continued walking slowly and deliberately down the path, scanning the hundreds of headstones that somewhere in the back of her mind reminded her of the endless rooftops she would see as she looked out the window of her art studio. The small dirt path took a long, sweeping turn to the left. Her determined stride was outwardly strong and deliberate. Breathing deep, she pressed on and on.

As she approached him, she stopped suddenly and looked straight up into the cloudless, blue sky, shutting her eyes tightly as if to hold the tears in. All she could hear was the distant traffic from the highway and the sounds of Mother Nature around her. The chiggers and crickets whirred and sang along with the distant traffic. After this briefest pause, Juju walked over to him, head hung low, looking almost sheepish.

"Hi, Sid," she said, struggling to get out just those two simple words. She looked around to see if anyone had heard her, but no one had. There was no one else in sight, and she was alone with Sid. She took a big gulp of warm summer air. "Oh, Sidney," she whispered harshly.

She fell to her knees in front of him and began to weep. A dark cry. A cry from somewhere deep in the pool of her soul, where the light was no longer allowed to reach. A cry only a young widow would understand. A cry only a young widow *could* understand. A cry that widowed women for generations, upon generations, have felt for their lost men.

She gasped and tried to catch her breath as the tears and rage started to pour out of her. "Sidney!" she screamed a little louder. She stopped crying and started wailing as she looked to the sky, and her hands squeezed the freshly turned soil. On her knees, she cried, screamed, and prayed to a God she no longer knew or cared to know. She fell forward, lying on his grave. Her cries echoed through the cemetery and carried on and on.

How long did she stay with him? Who knows? A minute? An hour? With finality, she got up and brushed her knees off, and with desolate conviction, she kissed the center of her palm and slowly blew her soft kiss to Sid.

"I love you, Sidney Apple," Ju whispered. She stood up straight and started the walk back up the thin dirt path to her car like a fighter after losing the championship fight. Her legs felt heavy, and her bones felt like they were made of stone. Her face was puffy, her eyes were red from crying, and her ribs hurt from sobbing and screaming. She wanted to lie down under the big oak tree at the end of the path and sleep. Maybe she would wake up, and Sidney would be lying next to her, stroking her hair and kissing her soft lips.

The walk back seemed to take forever. When she finally made it to her car, she paused and took a long look around the cemetery at the hundreds of stones dotting the lush, green acres. The obvious dawned on her, and she realized she wasn't alone. Cold comfort for the young widow. She slid into the driver's seat, wiped her eyes, and blew her nose. With a certain finality, she took a glance at the big oak tree and sighed lightly. She slowly drove back to her empty house to face the rest of the day alone.

CHAPTER 13

J immy sat on his back patio, turned to the late afternoon sun. This late July day, like every other day since Kristy died, seemed to drag out and on forever. Somewhere in the distance, he could hear children playing. It was a constant laughter dancing through the trees. As the streetlights come to life, they would head home for the night, their laughter following them home. In an instant, this fact took Jimmy back to his happy childhood, and a wisp of a smile crossed his face.

With a deep breath, he stood up and put his hands on his hips. He felt like moving; his body was crying out for exercise, and why not right now? He hadn't biked or gone for a run since, well, July third. And he was starting to feel loose and slightly out of shape. He turned around and looked toward the back door, wanting to tell Linda he was going to walk to the apple orchard; then with an internal shrug, he thought, it didn't matter.

So Jimmy walked alone through the woods behind the modest house he and Kristy had shared. He picked up a long stick on the side of the well-worn trail and examined it closely. A fine walking stick indeed! He walked slowly in deliberate steps through the familiar woods, along the familiar trail. It felt good to get out of the house.

The intentions of well-wishing family and friends were appreciated, but after so many days, Jimmy was growing tired and slightly annoyed with Linda for screening all the people who came to see him. Every day the house was filled with people. Some Jimmy knew, some he didn't. Jimmy was always polite and listened to their condolences with patience and understanding. He thought he did an outstanding job of hiding his urge to scream as loud as he could, wishing the world and all the people in his house would go away.

Jimmy made his way through the woods, enjoying the quiet solitude. He spoke aloud sometimes, sometimes in his head. He talked to Kristy while all the busy creatures, oblivious to him and his grief, went on with their happy, little lives. He walked up a small rise at the end of the woods that opened up into a largely abandoned apple orchard. Although no longer maintained, the trees still bore their fruit. He stopped, leaned against his walking stick, and closed his eyes. She had been gone for almost three weeks now. Three horrible weeks.

"Fuck," he mumbled to himself.

The just-barely-setting sun was warm and comforting. It was late July, but Jimmy could feel fall waiting in the wings, waiting to make its grand appearance. After a long, drawn-out minute of taking it all in, he began to walk through the apple orchard.

He started thinking about the first time he kissed her. It seemed so long ago. Then the obvious thought struck him rather strongly that he would never kiss her again. He would never hold her soft face in his hands and gently pull her close for a kiss. He sighed deeply and kept walking up through the orchard. As he walked, he knew he needed the season to change. Even after only a few weeks, the hot summer was a constant reminder of the day she died. Yes, he needed that change, badly. He leaned back again and felt the sun on his face. He began to think about his new life. This new fucking life.

Jimmy knew the change would be helpful. Would this be one of the hundreds of small turning points in his new and scary life? Some primal urge to start to heal perhaps? Was it possible that the same primal urge that drove grief today could heal it tomorrow? He gazed upward to the sky. Autumn would be here soon, like an old friend; and when the time came for change, he would open the door and welcome it in.

The walk through the orchard, dealing with his thoughts, had spun out a bit. Jimmy looked at his watch; it was getting late. "Shit," he said under his breath. He started back down the path to his house, ready to do battle with his new world, one more time at least.

As he came through the backyard gate, Linda stood in the doorway, holding a cup of coffee, waiting for him.

"There you are," she said, slightly relieved. "I didn't know where you went. I was worried."

"I'm fine," Jimmy said. "I just went up to the apple orchard to clear my head a little. Plus, I needed the exercise. Are you hungry? Who's still here? Anyone?"

Linda shook her head and took a small sip. "No, everyone left. Do you want to go out and get something to eat?"

Jimmy thought for a second. "Yeah, why not? Let me get cleaned up a little, and we'll go."

He stepped past Linda and went into his room to clean up and change. Linda frowned a little; she had a look of slight concern on her face.

As the warm days of July stubbornly ticked on and on, Jimmy watched family and friends slowly ease back into their lives. Summer was ending, and as much as he appreciated all the kindness and support, he was relieved when the steady exodus back to their well-wishing worlds began to give him the space to rebuild his.

The next day Linda prepared to go home. Jimmy sat up on the kitchen counter, watching silently as Linda finished making her morning coffee.

"Are you all packed?" Jimmy asked nonchalantly.

Linda shrugged as she walked to the fridge and opened it. "I guess so." She grabbed the milk, shutting the fridge with her hip. "Jimmy, I need you to tell me you'll be okay," she said without looking at him and trying not to get emotional. "I hate to worry about you, but you know I will."

"Linda, I'll be okay. I mean …" Jimmy trailed off, not quite sure what he wanted to say. He sighed, crossed his arms, and said, "Linda, thank you for everything and for being the gatekeeper here since the funeral. I got this now. Now I need time alone."

Linda got teary eyed despite her best efforts not to. "Jimmy, being here helped me too. Thank you. My sister loved you so very much. You know that, don't you?"

Jimmy sniffed and said, "I do. I know she loved me" as he lowered his eyes and repeated the words quietly like a prayer.

Ten minutes later, Jimmy was loading Linda's bags into the car and saying his goodbyes. "You call when you get home, okay? No speeding either," he joked lightly.

They hugged and said a quick goodbye. Jimmy stood in the driveway and watched her drive away until she took the corner and disappeared around the bend. He drew a deep breath, went back into the suddenly empty house, and shut the door.

Jimmy cocooned himself in his little house for the rest of the summer and fall, and he tried to heal as best he could. The weeks and months began to slowly and patiently tick on and on while he waited for the great change to wash over him.

CHAPTER 14

Juju, wounded and spent, wanted to be alone, too. The sympathy calls and visits were beginning to wear on her. So many times she wanted to retreat to her inner world with just her and Max. She wanted to be alone, to go far away to lick her wounds and rest. She wanted to start to heal.

Months later as the weather turned, Juju rolled her eyes and flipped the calendar attached to the refrigerator to December. She was already dreading Christmas and New Year's Eve too. She knew her friends and family would try to huddle around her and comfort her, but she knew already that she needed to be alone. As much as she appreciated them looking out for her, she knew this was something she needed to do. Was it part of the healing process? She didn't know or care. What she did know was that she needed to deal with this on her terms, and that meant being alone.

So Juju spent Christmas Eve alone. She watched the snow silently fall outside her front window, and the Pittsburgh weather forecast called for more. A white sheet of snow blew gently around her house, covering everything in a thick, white blanket. She spent most of the day cleaning the house while trying to occupy her mind with thoughts that didn't involve Sidney. She watched a movie and read a few chapters in the book she was tackling. It was a wonderful murder mystery about a set of twins who witnessed the brutal murder of a local shopkeeper, set in 1880s Boston.

At last, night settled in, and the entire house was dark except for the glow of the Christmas tree in the corner and a few small lamps, which adorned the living room. She sat on the floor close to the tree, with her legs crossed and a photo album on her lap. She cried openly, and the tears streamed down her cheeks as she slowly flipped the pages of the album. She stopped flipping the pages when she came to a picture of her and Sidney, which had been taken while they were in Alaska three years ago. The light from the Christmas tree cast a soft hue on the photo. Her fingers slowly touched the picture. She pulled it out of the plastic sleeve, held it close to her face, and closed her eyes as tight as she could. She dropped the photo onto her lap and put her hand over her mouth as if to stifle the scream that so badly wanted to come out. After a second she put the other hand over her mouth as if she needed both hands to hold in the scream.

Finally, the grief overcame her, and the screams of agony filled the empty, dark house. She sat on the floor with her head tilted upward to the ceiling, and the emotions poured out of her in long-drawn bawls of agonizing grief. She fell to her side and lay on the floor. "Oh, Sidney. Please, please, please come home," she begged in a choked, tearful voice, pleading to an unknown and unseeing spirit. "Oh, Sidney, pleeeeease!"

Eventually, Juju found sleep. She slept in dreamless peace, oblivious to the wind and snow blowing around the eaves of her house. She woke in the middle of the night and reached over to see whether this had all been a bad dream and whether Sidney was lying there next to her.

CHAPTER 15

The snowstorm blanketing Pittsburgh and Jujus house also pummeled Jimmy's house in Struthers. He watched the snow fall outside as Christmas carols floated in the air through the dimly lit house. He sat stony faced at the kitchen table, with a cup of soursop tea in front of him, which had long gone cold. A white blanket of snow covered the street, the trees, and the entire neighborhood.

He hurt badly tonight. It was Christmas Eve, and they were supposed to be together, running from house to house, making an appearance, eating, and moving on to the next relative's house.

He looked over at the poor excuse for a tree, with no presents under it this year. With a sad smile, he remembered the tree Kristy would trim—so full of life and color. Now the tree seemed sad and desperate like a strange reflection of himself. He finally gave up and retired for the night. He went into the bathroom to brush his teeth and took a long look at himself in the mirror. Even though he didn't know for sure, he thought he had lost weight. His appetite seemed to have left him completely. He took a closer look at himself and thought, *This is no way to run a ship.*

He slowly climbed into bed and curled up on his side. Kristy's side of the bed, as usual, lay untouched. He lay still, listening to the sharp wind blowing outside. He missed her so much. He felt as though he were perhaps slipping. He knew grief was a tough thing to control, but lately, he'd been saying to himself firmly, "One day at a time, Jimmy. You made it through today, and you'll make it through tomorrow, too. You'll see. It's going to get better. It *has* to get better because it can't get any worse. It just can't get any worse."

After twenty minutes of constant tossing and turning, Jimmy sighed and crawled out of bed. He walked to the bedroom window and looked out onto the side yard. Jimmy noticed a deer, so he stood perfectly still and watched with amazement as the deer lowered itself just slightly, then bolted across the yard in huge leaping bounds through the fresh-powdered snow. After a minute, Jimmy crawled back into his bed. It was a long time before he found sleep, and when he did, his sleep was thin.

The next morning Jimmy woke up and thought about that deer. Where did it go? Where do deer sleep? *I wish I could run like that deer!* Jimmy always felt better while moving, and with snow outside, those long bicycle rides were out. So he thought maybe he would take up cross-country skiing. Some fun and exercise were the perfect medicine right now. He laughed to himself, thinking Kristy must have planted that thought.

It was Christmas Day, so Jimmy got out of bed and decided what better time to buy some skis as a present. Love and kisses, Kristy.

CHAPTER 16

The winter was taxing on Juju. She visited her art studio only a handful of times, mostly just to check on things and make sure the heat was working. Sometime in early February, she walked in the icy rain to her studio, unlocked the big doors, and went in. She stood at the windows, looking at the dismal Pittsburgh skyline, which was barely visible in the rainy February afternoon.

She grabbed a brush and looked at it for a long time. She wasn't ready for this. She just wasn't ready to create anything while still dealing with everything she knew had been destroyed. Not yet anyway.

She put the brush back in its holder and walked over to the big, blank canvas leaning against the back wall. Untouched and unused, she touched it with the tips of her fingers. *Soon, old friend. Soon.*

Juju decided to spend some winter weekends on a friend's farm in Washington, Pennsylvania, who had invited her there to learn how to snowmobile. Not sure at first, she surprisingly found snowmobiling endlessly enjoyable. Juju lifted her goggles, her breath coming out in small, frosty puffs, looking at the cold world around her. Out in the rural surroundings of Pennsylvania, not a single creature was stirring for miles.

Juju closed her eyes and screamed as loud as she could into the darkening sky, her voice echoing across the barren fields of ice and snow. With a smidge of bravado, she lowered her goggles, climbed back on her snowmobile, and headed to the farm for a glass of brandy by the fireplace with good friends.

Life was getting better. Little by little, life was getting better.

As winter eventually succumbed to the will of Mother Nature and spring began to slowly take her place in the long and endless cycle of seasons, little by little the days got longer, and the air grew just a little warmer. Now the sun felt noticeably different, and once again a great and timeless change was at hand.

Spring made her grand entrance with a string of beautiful days, which sent the city of Pittsburgh into a whirlwind of activities. Downtown was full of tourists and locals, all out enjoying the warm days at Point State Park and flooding the area around Station Square. The huge fountain at Point State Park was now being cleaned and painted, and a flurry of groundskeepers were turning the gardens around the great lawn. From the fountain, if she looked across the mighty Allegheny River, she could see the lights at PNC Park flickering on and off as the crews replaced the huge bulbs that had gone bad over the winter. Baseball season was approaching, and Pirate hopefuls chatted about the new season over beers in the local pubs.

Juju was no different from other Pittsburgh locals, who wanted to get out and get busy. She got up early and ran to the garden center to load up on flowers and lawn garb to adorn her little house on Mount Washington. Her arms were full as she danced her way across the parking lot to her car. A little gasp escaped her when she realized for the first time in a long time that she was happy.

She came home, put on her gardening clothes and her hat and gloves, and got to work. As she started getting her flower beds ready for planting, she thought about how happy she felt now. The sun felt good on her neck, and the air was fresh and full of life. She made a mental note to tell Max about her observations.

The topper of the day was when Ju got a call from her agent, Devon, about a newly commissioned painting for an amazing client in New York City. She had told Dev last summer that she needed a complete break from work for a while and asked Dev to give her space and explain to potential clients that she was on sabbatical for the fall and winter. Clients were of course understanding and agreed to wait until spring. Juju was ready and very excited to start this new project he had gotten for her. She wrote on an old napkin as Dev spoke, "Paris scene. Winery."

Ju had put her career on hold when Sid started to get too sick to take care of himself. She had been a working artist for most of her life and had enjoyed huge success as such. Her art was well known in cities like New York, London, and Miami. Her work hung in homes, offices, and galleries. When she was just nineteen, the mayor of Pittsburgh had asked her to paint a piece in watercolor that showcased the city from the North Shore. That piece of art now hung in the Heinz History Center. Perhaps not her best work, but it was a piece she was most proud of.

She now spent the day planting her roses, fixing all the little things around the house that needed fixing, and daydreaming about her trip to the Big Apple. Yes, perhaps her new world was at hand.

CHAPTER 17

Jimmy opened his front door and took a deep breath of fresh spring air. Clad in his favorite shorts and T-shirt, he jumped down from his stoop and made his way to the garage. He smiled a little as he pulled his bike off the wall to begin the tedious, yet enjoyable, task of oiling up his old friend for his first ride of the year.

As he methodically and carefully began cleaning the machine, his mind drifted as usual to Kristy. The small smile on his face began to grow with the thought of her leaning against the garage wall and watching him. She would make light and airy conversation, peppered with little jokes, which always made him laugh. Just as he was in a nice rhythm of cleaning and polishing, his cell phone rang. Jimmy stood up to reach for the phone.

"Hi, this is Jimmy," he answered.

The voice on the other end was that of a colleague from New York City, Marc Gabrielle. Jimmy leaned against the garage wall and listened intently for a minute, then finally spoke. "Sure, I can do the shoot. Can you e-mail me all the details, bios of the models, and all the locations?" Jimmy felt a little rush of excitement. Marc replied that he could, and the two made some small talk and hung up.

Jimmy sat back down and continued cleaning his bike. His mind started going through the scenarios for the bridal shoot Marc had just explained. In that instant, he knew a trip to New York would be the perfect thing for his slowly mending soul. Of course, he had done work in New York many times, but this would be the first time since—well, since July.

Jimmy got on his bike, feeling excited and newly invigorated as he rode through the city streets. His mind stayed focused on his trip to New York and on just how badly he now wanted to go. For the first time in a long time, he was looking forward to something. He had forgotten how great that feeling was.

Finally, something to plan for. A target.

Yes, he thought as he looked over his shoulder while making a wide right-hand turn. *I'm on my way back.* He knew the road was long, but he also knew he was determined and had Kristy whispering in his ear.

CHAPTER 18

Juju's attic art studio had an amazing and unobstructed view of downtown Pittsburgh. It was a big, open space. Clients and friends who visited were awestruck by its grandness. The view was especially jaw dropping in the evening as the setting sun lit the tops of the skyscrapers a brilliant orange and red. During a small, five-minute window, the buildings looked as though they were on fire. It was the kind of view that took people's breath away. The kind of view that, when they saw it for the first time, it made them gasp just a bit.

She easily welcomed most people into her private sanctuary with humble pride. She and Sidney had worked very hard to build the space, which was only a few blocks from their house. It was perfect for her. Huge canvases of art filled the back walls, and in the center of the studio was a large, wooden, paint-covered table, which she used to sketch and mix paints. Along the walls, huge shelves were filled with paints, brushes, and books. The place was cluttered, but in such a large space, she barely noticed. Juju's cat, Goobersmooch, roamed around the studio and could often be found lying in the splash of sunlight, which moved ever so slowly across the old, well-worn wooden floors of the studio.

Juju sat at the table, wearing her favorite painting overalls and a white-splattered T-shirt. Her red hair had been pulled up in a messy bun, with speckles of paint on her hands and face. She had been working all morning on the new piece for a client in New York City. It was a landscape scene of a winery outside Paris. The canvas was huge and impressive. So far, it was looking wonderful. Not for the first time that day, she wondered how she was going to ship the monstrous piece to Manhattan. She made a note to call Dev and figure out the shipping details.

She didn't dwell on that thought for very long. Now, she was distracted by the rough, developing art on the table, which put a little smile on her face. It was going to be a showcase piece for sure.

As she sat on her stool, holding her tea with two hands, she took one last sip, put her teacup down, and stood up, stretching. Her break was over. Walking over to the radio on the top shelf, she upped herself on her tiptoes and turned on the music. She walked to the canvas and quickly picked up her brush again. Her hand slowly, and with great natural precision, started to cover the canvas. A great and elegant pass of her brush began the cycle of creation. Her painting came easily. Her eyes slightly squinted as she dabbed the brush and created her work.

Juju had been painting and drawing for as long as she could remember. She felt lucky that both her parents and teachers had nurtured her natural talent. By the time she turned fourteen, she was drawing characters of people at Light Up night, a festival around Forbes Avenue in Pittsburgh. She would come home afterward with her pockets stuffed with five- and ten-dollar bills. Then her first real job had been as an illustrator for a local Pittsburgh magazine called *The Point*. At only sixteen years old, Juju was the youngest person ever on staff at the prestigious magazine.

She was back in her groove now. She barely noticed the Cowboy Junkies' song "Angel Mine" playing on the radio. Almost subconsciously her bare feet started tapping, and her hips began to sway with the rhythm of the song. After a few moments, she turned her head toward the radio, and the brush dropped to her side. She smiled a little bigger now, dancing with her hands above her head and her hips making slow circles. The kind of dance the exotic dancers did at the bars and clubs on Eighth

Avenue. She danced and danced as Goobersmooch watched from her sunspot on the floor while licking her paw.

Juju let the time slip away while dancing and painting, and was surprised by how late it had gotten. She dropped her brushes in the sink, closed her paints, washed her hands, and took one last look at the almost-completed piece. She put on her sneakers, flipped off the lights and the radio, locked the door, and left.

It was a quick walk to her house, less than five minutes, door to door. She slipped in, went to the refrigerator, grabbed the container of orange juice, and took a long drink. She went to her bedroom, took off her overalls and T-shirt, tossed them down the basement steps, and was about to jump in the shower when the phone rang. "Shit," she muttered under her breath and instantly realized she hadn't brought her phone into the bathroom. Naked, she dashed into her room and looked at the screen. It read, "Dev London."

Standing there naked and feeling strangely vulnerable, Ju answered the phone. "Hi, Dev."

"How's the girl?" Dev asked in his thick British accent.

"I'm fine. To what do I owe the pleasure?" She stood there, feeling somewhat exposed, with her legs crossed and her forearm across her breasts, holding her phone in the other hand.

Dev asked, "Can you come to New York when your piece arrives and meet the clients to make sure the installation goes okay? I know it's short notice, but can you swing it?"

Juju raised her eyebrows and shrugged. "Yeah, sure. That is a good idea."

"Okay, great, and lovey, I just got off the phone with a courier company, and they will deliver the painting, Just have it packed and ready to go," Dev continued in his British accent. "You call me when you get to New York, righto."

"I will for sure, and thanks, Dev. It had completely slipped my mind to ask you about shipping it to New York," Juju said, switching the phone from ear to ear and chuckling.

Dev chimed in, "I'm reading your mind, Ju. It's all arranged. Enjoy New York. Cheers."

Ju said goodbye and comically ran into the bathroom.

As Ju showered, it dawned on her that a trip away from Pittsburgh was just what she needed. Her head was filled with ideas and plans as she ran through a quick mental itinerary. Maybe she would stay a few extra days. Perhaps? She considered her lodging and thought about the Geddy Hotel, a place she had read about; she'd always wanted to stay there. She needed an Amtrak ticket and maybe a new outfit for the day she delivered the piece. She also made note to call Sid's cousin, who lived in Queens with his wife and two kids. She hadn't seen them since the funeral and thought it might be nice to visit.

Juju stepped out of the shower and grabbed the towel hanging on the rack next to the toilet. She dried off, wrapped the towel around her, and grabbed her toothbrush. She stared at the fogged-up mirror for a moment, the toothbrush hanging loosely in her mouth. She lifted her hand and wrote "Sidney" on the foggy mirror. She stepped back for a minute to look at her "scrib." She bit her lip and smiled.

Juju hurried into her bedroom, dropped the towel, and put on her bra and underwear. Her toothbrush was still in her mouth, and she intermittently brushed as she got dressed. She jumped on the edge of her bed and put on her favorite socks. She scooted herself back to the bathroom and stuffed Q-Tips in her ears as she stared at the note on the mirror, vigorously finished brushing her teeth, spit in the sink, and looked back up at the note. She put her hand up to swipe it clean, paused for a second, then wiped it away.

In a few hours, Juju was meeting friends at her favorite downtown restaurant. It had been a while since she got dolled up and went out. She was feeling good today. Alive. It's said that when a person grieves, he or she goes through cycles. Juju didn't know whether that was true, but today she felt good, and she certainly wasn't going to argue about it. That night at dinner, surrounded by friends, she smiled over and over.

CHAPTER 19

Juju waited impatiently for her Uber to arrive to take her to the Amtrak station for her eight thirty train to New York City. She stood in her driveway with her oversized backpack slung loosely over her shoulder, shifting her feet back and forth; it was a nervous habit she had developed sometime in her early teens. She'd stayed up ridiculously late the night before, packing up the painting in a wooden frame with padded corner and waiting for the courier to pick up at her studio and drive it to New York, where she would meet the package.

She had managed only about two hours of sleep, but she took comfort in knowing she would be able to sleep on the train to New York. She knew that with her extremely petite size, she was easily able to curl up on the two side-by-side seat and sleep comfortably. She assumed the train would be relatively empty and would have no one sitting next to her.

The morning was gray and dismal in Pittsburgh, and the forecast called for clouds with a chance of rain. The early spring wind blew the budding leaves around her as she stood in her driveway. The world looked as if someone had brushed all the color out of it with the stroke of his or her hand. The bleakness of the early morning blanketed her. She sighed, looked down at her feet, and was thankful for the splash of color her red Converse shoes seemed to provide the otherwise-temporary gray Pittsburgh world.

Craning her neck at each set of oncoming headlights, she became anxious. She didn't care for tardiness. She heard her grandfather's words in her head. "Ju, if you're on time, you're already late." Wise words from a wise man.

Juju checked her watch again. 7:50. As if she had somehow telepathically summoned the car, she saw the Uber come slowly down her street. She held her hand up to get the driver's attention. The driver saw her and sped up to where she was standing. Ju opened the door and slid in. "Hiya!"

The Uber driver grunted and asked, "The Amtrak station?"

Looking at her phone to check the fare, Juju said, "Umm, yes, the Amtrak station on Forbes, please."

The Uber scooted easily through the tight streets of Mount Washington and on toward the train station. The driver was experienced and had no problem weaving through the Monday- morning traffic around Station Square. Juju watched out the window as a slight, misty rain began to fall, which seemed to dampen her mood. She sighed and looked at her happy red shoes again, which cheered her up, if only for a moment.

Crossing the Smithfield Bridge into downtown, Ju looked out to see the big coal barges on the river through the haze of rainy fog. She had seen those barges her entire life while growing up in Pittsburgh. Her dad had brought her and her brother, Matt, down to the river so many times when they were young to watch the boats. Juju, who had been maybe ten years old at the time, fondly remembered her dad teaching her how to skip rocks while watching the barges slowly drift by. Ten minutes later, the driver pulled into the station.

Juju gathered her backpack, stepped out of the car, and thanked the driver. She walked into the station, past the lobby, and up the stairs to the platform. She found an open seat on the bench and sat to wait for the boarding call, smiling at her red shoes. Just as she settled in, a robotic voice announced all passengers should board, so Juju made her way to the business class car. She climbed the three steps and quickly found a seat. With great relief, she observed the car was almost empty, so her fears of not being able to lie down instantly vanished. Fifteen minutes later, the train started its long trip to New York City. Juju settled in for the long ride and was happy she was tired. The train could be boring depending on her mindset, and Ju relied on sleeping through any boredom she faced. She was one of those fortunate people who was able to sleep anywhere.

Ju glanced out the window with heavy eyelids and was able to see Kennywood across the river. She smiled nostalgically, remembering the many hours she had spent at the famous Pittsburgh amusement park as a kid and all the times she had gone there with Sid. On one memorable occasion, they went with a group of their closest friends, drank Iron City beer in the parking lot, and got too drunk to go inside the park. They all ended up ordering pizza and crashing in the back of Sidney's best friend's pickup truck.

She remembered the time she went on the Steel Phantom roller coaster with Sidney, then threw up in the bushes as soon as they got off. *Oh my God, how we both laughed so hard!* Sidney picked her up and carried her to the nearest bench, where she sat while he ran to get her a lemonade. She remembered leaving the park at closing time, hand in hand with Sid, and both looking up at the heart-shaped sign, which said, "Good Night."

All ghosts that haunt the mind aren't scary and bad, she thought. The smile stayed locked on her mouth as the train sped forward and the iconic amusement park slipped away in the gray Pittsburgh fog.

Despite her exhaustion, Ju found herself feeling antsy and unable to sleep until the big silver train sped past Altoona. Finally, she lay down across the two seats and adjusted herself. The steady hum of the train put her asleep in a relatively short time. The conductor came by, looked at her curled up and sleeping, checked the stamp on her ticket to New York City, and moved on.

The train rushed ahead eastward with the afternoon sun at its back. The horn gently echoed through the central Pennsylvanian hills like some strange haunting spirit calling out. The sky quickly turned from gray to brilliant blue as if God's breath had gently blown the gray away. Through all this, Juju slept on and on.

The next day, Ju called Sidney's family in Queens and arranged to spend the day visiting with them. They went to the zoo, and had a huge, wonderful backyard barbecue. This was the first time in a long time that she truly enjoyed herself. They all laughed while talking about Sid and all the wonderful memories they had of him. She had always loved Sid's extended New York family, and of course, they loved her.

Sid's cousin Tabatha walked Ju to the subway station, where they said their goodbyes, and Ju promised to try to come to New York more often. The train pulled into the station, and Juju jumped on. She gave a little wave to Tabatha and and blew her a kiss as the train sped off into the Queens night, bound for Manhattan.

CHAPTER 20

The alarm buzzed, and Jimmy made several half-hearted attempts to turn it off before finally swinging his legs out of bed. He took a minute to gaze out the bedroom window to meet the dawn. He sniffed, rubbed his eyes, and stretched out on his tiptoes.

The ride to the train station in Pittsburgh was about an hour, but he always gave himself extra time for traffic and other unexpected delays. He mentally went through the checklist of things he needed for the trip. Phone, wallet, glasses, iPad, his backpack, and so on. He had dropped Taffy off at Kristy's mom's place the night before, and now he was glad he did. He didn't want to go twenty minutes out of the way to drop the dog off this morning. The house alarm beeped twice as he closed the front door.

He stopped on his front porch and tasted the early-morning dew. He breathed the cool, clean spring air in deep and let it sit on his tongue. With this taste of new life, Jimmy jumped off the front porch, landed on the grass, and jogged to his car. He was in an especially good mood. Perhaps it had something to do with spring finally making its grand entrance and freeing him from the miserable, cold grip of winter. Whatever the case, he was excited and anxious to get his trip started to New York City.

He made awesome time getting to Pittsburgh. Traffic was light in the city, so he was able to swing into a Quickie Mart to pick up some light snacks for the train ride to New York.

Taking a sip of the three-dollar water, he kicked himself for not being the super genius who had thought of selling free water to the masses. After all, when he looked at the bottle, the name Evian was *naive* spelled backward, he mused, smiling to himself.

Jimmy sped down Fort Duquesne Boulevard to Eleventh Street and swung into the parking deck across from the train station. He circled up and up, finally picking a safe spot on Lou Gehrig, level four. The Iron Horses number. He glanced in the rearview mirror and watched a young couple, hand in hand, walking through the garage from the elevators. The familiar ping of the girl's high heels clicking through the garage brushed him like a melancholy breeze of his late wife. He quickly shook it off, opened the door, grabbed his bags out of the back, and walked to the elevators.

As he climbed the steps to the train platform, he noticed the long line at the ticket counter. *Why don't people just buy their tickets online and save some trouble?* he thought, shaking his head. At the top of the stairs, there were several rows of wooden benches in the small waiting area. Most were full by now, so Jimmy found a spot on the wall and waited for them to announce the boarding of business-class passengers. He looked around and was amused by the wide variety of people, who chose to ride the train. Maybe like him, they enjoyed the nostalgia of the train ride, too.

Yes. The train was quintessential Americana—riding the rails across Pennsylvania, New Jersey, and New York; looking out the dirty train window; seeing moment by moment as intimate worlds brush by in a splash of old-school Technicolor. The pink flamingos and junk cars in the yards. The drips and drabs of old, discarded toys tossed carelessly on the sides of tilted garages. Rural farmhouses looking as if they were hexed or haunted. During the fall, those same farmhouses were adorned with witches, pumpkins, and goblins as the dead, brown leaves blew across the unkempt grass to disappear in the empty fields of corn. The chilly autumn sun, setting over the silos in the distance, signaled that strange and ageless feeling of dread. That feeling would send shivers down his spine as the flickering candles in the windows of the farmhouses, like stars on a starless night, were the only defense protecting him from all the scary things children feared during Halloween. Yes. Jimmy loved it all.

Right on time, the PA announced the boarding of the business class passengers, snapping Jimmy out of his haze. He picked up his bags, headed out to the big silver train, and climbed aboard. Organizing his laptop, papers, and books, he kept his fingers crossed that no one would sit next to him or anywhere near him for that matter. The little act of ancient luck worked, when fifteen minutes later the train jolted forward, and Jimmy sat alone.

He spent most of the morning going over the details of the shoot on Thursday. He looked at the headshots of the models and went over the itinerary for the day. The schedule was going to be tight, but that was fine with him, since he seemed to work better with deadlines. For the rest of the day, he engulfed himself in a novel about the Civil War. He stopped reading long enough to eat lunch and dinner, and to make some phone calls, but other than that, the book kept him lost and enthralled. Frequently, he paused and looked out the window at the passing scenery, always curious about the people in all the houses and what they might be doing at that exact moment. A story in every window. This thought always made him smile.

As evening started to knock, Jimmy stretched and thought about a little sleep. He pulled his jacket out of his bag and rolled it up into a makeshift pillow. He stuffed it against the window and laid his head on it. He watched as the Amtrak conductor made his rounds up and then down the car, making chitchat with a small, seemingly select group of privileged riders, like a bartender making chitchat with his regulars. Jimmy gave it a small, almost cynical, smile. *When did I become so cynical?* He heard Kristy whisper in his ear, "That, Jimmy, is an excellent photograph of Americana."

The conductor gave Jimmy just a slight nod, and Jimmy nodded back. The conductor glanced up at his ticket attached to the luggage rack, making sure it was stamped for New York's Penn Station, and moved along. A long moment later, the conductor dimmed the lights, and the car took on that yes, very Norman Rockwell-ish soft glow. Jimmy smiled. Kristy was always right.

It was quiet except for the steady hum of the train, broken only by the occasional echoing horn as they glided through rural Pennsylvanian towns. Jimmy's heart beat to a slow rhythm as he glanced out the window at the dimly lit attics in the rowhouses that passed by, like a 1920s flicker show at some mystical nickelodeon. His thoughts of Kristy come easily now, wrapped up in this vibrating hum of the engine. He missed her so much. In that sacred space between wake and sleep, he remembered … he remembered everything. How she loved "Clair de Lune." He had heard the soft Debussy fill the house on warm summer afternoons like he was hearing it now in his dream.

In his mind's eye, she sat by the window and stared out into the yard with her gentle brown eyes, gazing upward from time to time to see the lofty, floating clouds of early summer. Oh, how she loved the clouds! Her soft hands were wrapped around her favorite coffee cup. Jimmy was leaning in the kitchen doorway, watching the summer sun make slow circles in her long brown hair. She was at the peak of her life. She was at the peak of her *being*. Her face was passive and calm. She turned to him and smiled. That smile … oh, that smile.

Jimmy's eyes closed now, his body gently rocking with the sway of the train. A slight smile grew on his face. He dreamed easily now. He dreamed of her.

CHAPTER 21

Juju sat by the window in her room, watching the sun leave the city from the Twenty-Fourth floor of the Geddy Hotel. She had deliberately turned off the lights to give her a better view of New York at night. From up here, the city below truly looked like some wonderful painting that had come to life in front of her. It was almost surreal to think about. It was the kind of strange beauty that made her feel drunk and dizzy.

She sat in the oversized chair she had pulled close to the window. The faint howl of sirens rolled through the canyons of the city below her like a lullaby. Her eyes were glazed and dreamy. It had been a long day, and she was quickly growing tired. She put her feet up on the windowsill and stretched her legs. She leaned forward, took off her lacey bra, and tossed it absently on to the floor.

Her passive face broke just slightly into a smile as she thought of Sidney. *Sidney*. She gazed with childlike wonder out at the city, remembering his warm kiss on her neck. His strong hands caressing her body, touching her breasts. She sighed sadly and deeply. "I miss you." She whispered so softly that she barely heard her voice in the dark, quiet room. Her body was now physically aching for his touch; she let her fingertips softly caress her breasts. After a long moment, she unbuttoned her pants and slid them down slowly, deliberately, and pulled one leg out. She spread her legs open on the windowsill. Her thoughts were now completely engulfed by long nights with her husband.

His hands on her body. His mouth on her mouth. With her feet still up on the sill, she let go, thinking of Sidney. Her orgasm came quick and strong. She could feel her slick fluid on the inside of her thighs. She bit her lip as she moaned softly, and her breath came out in jagged, little puffs in an exquisite release. She smiled.

With a sigh of secret satisfaction, Juju stood up, kicked off her pants, and went to the bathroom. As she walked to the mirror, she saw a quirky, little smile on her face. She laughed at herself and sat on the toilet with her elbows on her knees, her eyes closed. She felt a little better.

She put on a fresh pair of underwear and her favorite beat-up and tattered Rolling Stones T-shirt, brushed her teeth, and snapped off the light. She ran across the hotel room and jumped into the bed, something she'd done every night since she was a little girl. Climbing under the covers of the big, king-size bed, she curled up tightly.

She looked back out over the city, her eyes now heavy with sleep. Her mind had quickly slipped and spiraled into neutral. She blinked. She blinked. She blinked again, this time a long blink, and her eyes stayed shut. She dreamed easily now. She dreamed of him.

CHAPTER 22

The train arrived in New York hours behind schedule. Weaving his way through Penn Station, Jimmy grabbed a cab outside and took it to the hotel, where he quickly showered, unpacked, and climbed into bed almost immediately. He stayed up for a bit and watched the local New York news and the beginning of an old spaghetti western, which was amusingly bad. When he finally dozed off, his sleep was deep, dreamless, and still.

By morning the sun drenched his hotel room on Fiftieth Street and woke Jimmy. Swinging his legs out of bed, he sat on the edge, looking out over Manhattan. He rubbed his jaw with some displeasure at the three-day growth on his face. The stubble made him feel out of sorts and unwound. He scanned the city from sky to street. It was a beautiful day. As he stretched, rubbing his eyes, he looked around the bed for his phone, picked it up, and saw two new voice mails.

Jimmy listened to both messages without any fanfare. The first was from his sister in Phoenix. She was concerned about their father, who had made the announcement that he would be cutting his own lawn this spring and summer. Jimmy deleted the message with a slight look of irritation. The second message was from Marc, asking about the shoot tomorrow. He stood up and called him back.

"Hey, Marc!" Jimmy said.

"Jimmy!" Marc was genuinely happy to hear his voice. Although they hadn't known each other for very long, they had become fast and good friends. Jimmy smiled and always appreciated Marc's enthusiasm. "Are you in the city?" Marc asked.

"Yeah, got in late last night. The fucking train was like six hours late," Jimmy said with a slight chuckle.

Marc gawked, "Man, that sucks. If you got some sleep, wanna meet for lunch today?"

Jimmy countered, "How about dinner? I was going to go rent a bike and ride around a bit today. After that long train ride, I need to move these old bones a little!"

"Yeah, of course," Marc said. "See you tonight at seven o'clock at The Grace Cafe?"

"Is that the place on Twenty-Third?" Jimmy asked.

"Yep," Marc replied. "I'll meet you in front at seven then."

Jimmy hung up the phone and dressed in his biking clothes. He stretched a bit and filled his water bottles with New York's finest naive water, chuckling to himself. He pulled out his biking backpack and stuffed it with a cheap camera, some granola bars, and old maps of New York. He also threw in a pair of reading glasses and an extra pair of sunglasses. He hurried out the door and to the elevator. Minutes later he was walking quickly out of the main lobby doors toward Ninth Avenue and the bike shop, where he could rent his ride for the day.

CHAPTER 23

Juju stepped out of the cab on Park and Sixty-Second, and walked quickly down the sidewalk to the address she had scribbled on her palm. She was rushing to meet the courier to deliver the painting to her clients. She easily found the beautiful building, where the well-to-do Mr. and Mrs. Paul Como lived. After a quick Google search, Ju discovered the Como's owned the nation's largest wholesale electronics company. Juju sniffed and secretly thought she should have charged more.

As she stood there, looking for the van that had her painting, she felt her phone vibrate in her pocket. She looked at the screen. "Hello, Dev."

In an anxious British accent, Dev asked, "Are you at the apartment? Is the painting there yet? Did you find it okay?"

Juju rolled her eyes and answered. "Yes. No. And yes. Are you coming here?"

Dev said, "No. I have to catch a plane to London, doll. However, I do have some good news."

Juju raised her eyebrows. "Do tell."

Dev continued, "We have a new client for you. A steady high-end client. It's a sure thing, Ju. I'm meeting with them next week when I get back to New York. You'll have work lined up for a long time with this client; good work, Ju. You'll be set up."

Juju bit her lip and smiled. "Dev, that's awesome! I'm so excited!" She put her finger in her ear as a fire truck went by, sirens blaring. "Call me when you talk to them," she yelled into the phone.

"I will. Cheers, Ju!" And Dev hung up.

Just as she put her phone in her back pocket, a blue van slowly pulled up to the curb. Ju gave a little wave. "Are you Juju ... umm ... Apple?" The driver looked at the delivery invoice once more to make sure her name was really Apple and that he had read it correctly.

Juju nodded, and the driver rolled up the window and jumped out. Juju had a quick chat with the doorman, and they carefully took the painting to the penthouse apartment.

CHAPTER 24

Jimmy entered Denny's Bikes on Ninth Avenue. Over the last couple of years, he had gotten to know the staff fairly well at the shop, and he always rented from them when he was in the city. Bringing his own cycle from Struthers had been an option, but he found it easier to just rent a quality cycle from Denny's, and this allowed him the opportunity to try out different bikes. He spent most of the day cycling around Manhattan and Brooklyn. After all the cross-country skiing in the winter, he was in amazing shape and could easily do the fifty-plus miles he targeted. He did, however, stop often to see the sights and snap pictures of his adventure through the city.

Around noon he stopped in Washington Square Park for lunch. As he sat on the bench close to the fountain, he peeled off his backpack and pulled out a granola bar. A biker's lunch. He looked around to see the street performers who made the park their stage of choice. He would stop here often with Kristy on their trips to New York. Sometimes he felt like the entire world was haunted by her spirit. He surmised a lot of widowed people felt the same way.

Just then a group began gathering around some young street kids, who were all sitting around different-size buckets. They started to play buckets like drums. Their steady drumming, along with their hoots and hollers, quickly drew a crowd of eager tourists. It seemed as if they all had their cameras out and were taking pictures. The drummers played a syncopated beat for the crowd, and Jimmy watched all the feet tapping along to the drums. Another great photo.

After the fifteen-minute street show, Jimmy packed up his gear and headed back out on his bike toward Brooklyn. He spent the rest of his day riding around Dumbo, checking out the sights and sounds of New York. Just after four o'clock, Jimmy made his way back to Denny's to drop off the bike, then hurried back to the hotel to get showered and changed for dinner with Marc.

CHAPTER 25

Everything went perfectly when Juju delivered the painting to her clients. They gushed and raved about the finished work, while Juju stood by, beaming with artistic pride, as the painting was hung on the wall above the sofa. It set the room ablaze and looked amazing in its new home. She had a very nice-sized check in her pocket; plus her agent Dev had a meeting next week with another client who was also interested in her work. Things were starting to happen for her here in New York.

Juju's happy clients hugged her goodbye, and she decided to walk through Central Park. She walked slower than usual as the leaves from last fall blew gently around her.

While she was lost in nature's beauty, the city traffic was muted if only for a moment. Life was good. Life was *grand*. The sun splashed around her as she walked with her hands stuffed in her pockets past The Pond. She watched the little kids playing on the giant rocks, with parents keeping a close eye on their little ones. She cut up to Fifty-Ninth Street, past the line of horse and carriages parked and waiting for customers. She looked at the horses with a certain amount of empathy. As a lifelong vegetarian, she found their treatment mean and imagined them instead frolicking free on the great plains. She walked toward Columbus Circle, and her eyebrows raised in delight when she saw the street vendors cart selling ice cream cones.

"Can I have a chocolate ice cream cone, please?" Juju said. The nice man who served her the cone commented on how nice her smile was. She strutted a little at the compliment and made her way over to Columbus Circle. She saw a low brick wall in the shade and scooted over to it.

With her ice cream cone in hand, she jumped up on the wall. She had greatly underestimated her jumping skills and landed hard on her butt. Her teeth snapped together as she balanced her cone to keep it from tipping. "Fuck," she mumbled comically. Despite the newly forming bruise on her ass, it was indeed a good day.

CHAPTER 26

The following morning, Juju slept in until nine thirty or so and stayed in bed for a bit, feeling luxuriously lazy. She had the entire day to herself in New York City, so she flipped through the stations on TV and watched a few minutes of the local news. She loved the fact that she had nothing to do but have fun in the Big Apple.

With a huge stretch and yawn, she pulled herself out of bed and went to the window, seeing it was another wonderful spring day in the city. The sky was cloudless and brilliantly blue. The endless rows of buildings stretched on and on like a concrete canyon. She put her forehead against the glass window and stared out over the Hell's Kitchen neighborhood below. Just then, her phone beeped with a new e-mail. She walked over to the nightstand and looked at the screen. It was a message from yesterday's client. Her eyebrows raised as she touched the screen, and the e-mail popped up. She carefully read the message twice.

Hello, Juju

I just wanted to take a minute to thank you for the wonderful piece that you created for us. We are in love with it. You are an incredible talent, and we feel so blessed to have one of your pieces in our home.

We understand that you lost your husband, Sidney, not too long ago. We are incredibly sorry for your loss. Although we never met Sidney, with a fine person such as yourself as his wife, it speaks volumes to the kind of man he must have been. Our hearts break for you, and we hope God allows you to find peace in your ever-amazing heart.

Sincerely,
Paul and Constanza Como

Ju smiled hugely and was truly touched. Her clients were very busy people, and it didn't go unappreciated by Juju that they had taken the time to write this elegant e-mail of kind words. She could almost hear her dad whisper in her ear. "The world is a good place, Ju, full of good people." She agreed. She was proud of herself.

Ju went to the bathroom and turned on the shower. She kicked off her underwear, adjusted the hot water, and pulled off her Rolling Stones T-shirt, and jumped into the perfectly hot shower. She luxuriously stayed in the steam longer than usual. The hot water wasn't going to run out, and the pressure was strong: two qualities that made a great shower. She slid down the tiled wall and sat on the floor, letting the warm water cascade down on her like a waterfall. Finally, she stood up, rinsed her hair one last time, and turning the shower knobs off.

She pulled the big, fluffy white towel off the hook and wrapped herself in it. She grabbed another towel and wrapped up her hair. The bathroom steamed up the mirror, so she walked out into the living room and turned on the TV to cool off. She reached into her oversized backpack on the bed and pulled out her favorite and most comfortable jeans, a black, slightly oversized T-shirt, a pink bra and panty set, with matching pink socks, and of course, her red Chuck Taylors.

She quickly dressed and dried her hair, absentmindedly thinking she should buy a cute baseball hat today. Perhaps a really cute New York Yankees cap. Ju stood up, slipped on her jeans, and started flipping through the TV stations as she continued getting ready. All dressed and ready to go, she was happy with what she saw in the mirror. She had always liked her body and face. Humble self-esteem was not a problem with Juju Apple.

The doorman gave her a nice smile and tipped his cap as she bopped out the front door onto Forty-Fifth street. She decided to start her day by going down to the Brooklyn Bridge and seeing what she could see. She held up her hand and grabbed a cab. As much as she liked the subway, a cab seemed easier. Navigating the New York subway system can be a bit difficult. She knew the basics, at least, but that was it.

After seeing what she could see at the bridge, she suddenly realized she had skipped breakfast and was getting hungry. So she grabbed a cab to Soho to do a little shopping and snacking. She figured she could have lunch after she spent a little of her hard-earned money. She found her way into a dozen little specialty boutiques. She bought a scarf, a very cool pearl bracelet, and yes, a very cool Yankees baseball cap, which she put on as soon as she left the store. She also bought a pair of purple jeans and a polka-dot top she'd absolutely loved as soon as she saw it in the window.

A few blocks later, she drifted into an art gallery just to take a peek. Many of her pieces had been displayed and sold in galleries here in New York, London, Paris, and Los Angeles. She walked slowly through the gallery with her arms folded across her chest and her bags close. Two pieces made her stop, and she spent a few minutes looking at them. One depicted a woman walking in the rain and holding an umbrella, and the other was a postmodern piece of a skyline of light and water. She was drawn to and loved both wonderful pieces. Despite Juju being a sought-after artist, her love for art boiled down to its simplest form. She felt a good painting was a good painting. Style, education, experience—they were irrelevant. Love is love. If you loved a painting, you loved it. A good painting was a good painting, be it an art student or an Andy Warhol.

Juju was well aware that she wasn't the stereotypical fine artist who made her way around galleries in New York and London. In certain circles in the art world, she was a respected cutting-edge artist. It wasn't until you met her face-to-face that you realized she was an incredibly charismatic, funny, goofy person. People were drawn to her for both her artistic ability and her incredibly eccentric personality. She walked toward the door to leave, turning for one last look at the painting of the woman with the umbrella, then walked out into the sunshine.

She put on her trendy sunglasses, pulled her new, most awesome Yankees cap down just a little, and continued her walk. She loved the Soho neighborhood. It was her favorite New York City spot. It reminded her of London in so many ways. For that matter, she also loved London. Both cities were so rich in culture and art. They each seemed to have a pulse she could feel, whether she was walking down Broadway in New York City or one of the countless and timeless cobblestone side streets in London. It was like the people left their energy behind, vibrating in the stone.

Juju walked onto Thompson Street, thinking about London. Five years ago she had gone there with her bestie, Cheryl, for one of Juju's art shows. They'd had so much fun dressing in 1970s London garb. Their first stop was Pollywogs, the trendy retro boutique. They both burned up their credit cards and some of Ju's commission check on ultra-fun fashion. They wore bell-bottom, low-cut pants that showed off their stomachs and hips, and floppy hats they would wear only in London. They both resembled Twiggy knockoffs, strolling through London's fashion district, sometimes hand in hand.

After a nice lunch, she hailed a cab to the hotel to drop her bags and rest for a bit. She was looking forward to spending the rest of the day at The Met. She loved walking through the halls of the famous museum, taking in all the exhibits and wonderful pieces of art. She was looking forward to a nice dinner and a quiet evening back at the hotel.

CHAPTER 27

It was a long yet fulfilling day for Jimmy at the photo shoot in Brooklyn. The shoot itself went very well, and Jimmy was extremely pleased with the preliminary results he saw. He felt confident his clients would be pleased, too.

He made his way back from the Dumbo neighborhood in Brooklyn to his hotel in Manhattan by Uber, quickly showered, and changed his clothes. He called down to the front desk and asked the nice concierge if anyone could recommend a good vegetarian restaurant, maybe within walking distance of the hotel. She knew of a great vegan restaurant just a couple of blocks away, so Jimmy scratched down the name and address, put on his favorite New York Yankees cap, and headed out into the city. He walked the six blocks until he found the restaurant the hotel recommended. The green-and-white marquee said, "Leaf" in plain, bold script. He laughed, thinking, *Well, that sounds vegan.*

A young, hippy-looking hostess at the podium, with an abundance of colorful tattoos, asked how many, and Jimmy replied, "Just me." The hostess smiled at Jimmy as they walked through the semi-crowded restaurant. He touched her arm and asked whether he could sit at one of the tables outside. She smiled and led him to an open table on the patio facing Fifty-Fourth Street. He sat down and pulled out his phone, checking to see whether Marc had called or whether he had received any new messages. Nope.

Jimmy enjoyed his solitary dinner of pasta and mushrooms. He didn't mind eating alone. It was as if some distant part of him rather enjoyed the blank solitude from time to time. He noticed that even in a city like New York, it was possible to be alone and reclusive without drawing any particular attention to himself.

In the time since Kristy died, he had started to enjoy his alone time more and more. He wondered silently whether the strange urge to be alone was a by-product of his grief or just his internal psyche changing with age. He quickly decided he didn't care one way or the other. In no hurry to get back to the hotel, he decided to order dessert, a fruit dish with blueberries, strawberries, and pomegranate. Three of his absolute, all-time favorites.

As always, his mind seemed to wander in circles when given the chance. For a second, he let himself relive Kristy's funeral. He hung to the memory just long enough to feel the ever-so-slight push of tears, so he quickly switched gears and finished his dessert. He wasn't going to let himself slide down to that sad place tonight. Nope, not tonight. Any thoughts of Kristy were going to be good thoughts and good memories.

This choice was something Jimmy had been making a clear effort to do. When he thought of her, he tried to think of the happy times. The good times. He was trying to smile more and cry less, and strangely, he felt he was doing a better job at that now as the months and seasons slowly and steadily ticked by.

His family had nonchalantly suggested that he join one of those widower support groups. The thought of sitting in a church basement and listening to a bunch of old, grieving widow and widowers didn't exactly appeal to him. No, he would deal with things on his own time and schedule. If anyone asked him, he would always say he was doing just fine. He didn't need some pastor pretending to understand the ins and outs of his grief.

Fuck it. Fuck everyone. Including the fucking pastor.

After he paid the waitress, he got up and ducked into the bathroom to wash his hands.

It was a warm and pleasant spring evening in New York, so Jimmy started to walk up Fifty-Fourth Street toward Central Park. He loved the city, and he kept thinking about what Marc had said to him about moving here. He had always thought he would end up here eventually. Maybe in a few years, he would pack up and move to Manhattan, where he imagined himself in a little apartment in The Village somewhere close to Washington Square Park. During the week he could work on his fine art photography, and on the weekends he could shoot select weddings. He knew in a few years he wanted to curtail his busy wedding schedule to focus more time on his fine art and street photography. New York was the ideal place to do both. Someday.

There were still more than a couple of hours of daylight left, and Jimmy knew they played baseball games in the park, so he thought he would walk over and have a look. He was leaving for Pittsburgh tomorrow morning, so he wanted to make the most of his last hours in the city. Moments later he disappeared into the sea of people on the street, and he headed up Eighth Avenue toward Central Park. Wearing his Yankees cap, he walked to the park entrance at Columbus Circle and went right past the statue where Juju had sat yesterday in her Yankees cap, eating her ice cream cone and relishing the day and her sweet, sweet success.

He walked down the path past the fountains to the manicured baseball fields. His face lit up a little when he saw a game in full swing. The crack of the bat and screams from the sparse yet enthusiastic crowd warmed him and drew him to the field like a siren song.

Jimmy quickly found a seat on the mostly empty bleachers and sat down to watch the game. He had fallen in love with baseball about the same time he met Kristy. He always thought it funny that he'd discovered love and baseball slightly later in life. Jimmy sat with his elbows on his knees while watching the tail end of the game, remembering Kristy and how she had loved baseball too. They'd gone to Pittsburgh Pirates games frequently. They always left early to spend a couple of hours walking around Pittsburgh and enjoying the sights before heading over to the ballpark. They always had so much fun together, holding hands while walking around the city and people watching.

This game he was watching now was just the kind Kristy would have loved. He could picture her sitting next to him, eating popcorn, and occasionally asking him questions about the game as they rooted for their team together. He missed that he missed her. And right now he remembered how sexy she had looked wearing his new Pirates jersey on that fateful day.

The spring sun was just starting to dip through the trees on the west side of the park, casting a warm glow across the field. The game ended just as it was starting to get too dark to play anymore. Jimmy stood up and stretched, noticing the players all high-fiving, laughing, and cheering like they were all lifelong pals. He envied their camaraderie. Maybe that too was what he missed with Kristy. They had always been on the same team.

Jimmy jumped off the bleachers. He slowly made his way out of the park and back toward Eighth Avenue. He dipped into a bodega on Eighth and Fifty-Seventh and grabbed a copy of the *New York Post* and a bottle of orange juice for later that night. Still smiling from the game, he walked out the door, and in a quick moment, he decided to take the long way back to the hotel to look at the sights and window-shop the posh stores along Fifth Avenue. The New York City sunset streamed through the concrete canyons as he walked, and he took it all in.

At the hotel, he thanked the doorman for the recommendation of the fine vegan restaurant. Before Jimmy headed to his room for the night, they chatted for a moment about vegan food, the Mets, and the New York Yankees. His bags were all packed, with his clothes laid out for the train ride home to Pittsburgh the next morning. He spent an hour or so on the phone with Marc and one of the magazine editors, going over a few details of the shoot. Jimmy often gave his advice for layouts and which photos he thought were going to be the best for what the magazine was trying to put forth to its readers. They didn't always take his advice, but that didn't bother him that much. It just pleased him that they always asked for his creative input.

Finally, after hanging up the phone, he turned on the TV and crawled into bed. He found the Yankees on and watched as they clobbered the Red Sox in Boston. It was still relatively early, but he felt tired and spent after the long day. Not even the Yankees could keep him from sleep tonight. As he propped himself up to see the TV, he still thought about Kristy. He snacked on cookies he had gotten from the bodega, and as soon as he closed his eyes, sleep found him.

CHAPTER 28

J u was fast asleep, surrounded by pillows and blankets, with Max on her chest, opened to a blank page. Her long day of treasure hunting in Soho had worn her little body out. The sweet swirl of color magically spun itself into a dream in her sleeping mind. She was walking on a beach with a long fishing pole in her hand. For a brief second, her father was walking with her, smiling. Then he was gone. She stopped and called for him. "Daddy! Daddy!" But there was no answer. The only sound was the surf crashing all around her, with the sun warm and bright against her slightly pale face.

She dreamed she was casting the line out into the ocean like her father had taught her so many years ago. That breeze blew hard on her face, and her red hair twirled in circles in the wind. The sky quickly turned dark, and she could no longer see where the beach ended and the water began. She found herself panicking and drowning in the darkness, desperately swimming and looking for the beach that was no longer there. She tried in vain to scream for help, but nothing would come out.

In the dark and quiet room of the hotel, she thrashed the blankets off and moaned in her sleep. Without realizing it, she knocked her phone and a glass of water off the nightstand. Surprisingly, come morning she wouldn't remember the dream or how the phone and empty glass had ended up on the floor. She sat on the edge of the bed, looking down at them, perplexed and confused. She grabbed a quick shower, packed her backpack, and got ready to make her way to Penn Station.

Juju walked out of the Geddy Hotel lobby on Seventh Avenue, turning toward the station. It was a Friday morning, and the city sidewalks were busy with people, all walking quickly to points unknown. She thought about hailing a cab but quickly dismissed it. She was grudgingly aware that she was going to spend the next nine hours or so on a train; besides, it was another beautiful spring morning in Manhattan, so her step quickened a bit as the cool spring air turned her cheeks slightly rosy red.

She passed Thirty-Ninth, then Thirty-Eighth, Thirty-Seventh, and so on; and as she crossed Thirty-Third, she looked to her left and stole a long glance at the Empire State Building. She remembered that Sidney had loved that building. She grinned a little. She cut past the cab lines and found the big glass doors of Penn Station. She made her way down the steps inside, on time for her eight thirty train back to Pittsburgh. Dodging and weaving through the thousands of New Yorkers and tourists, who all seemed to be in a hurry, she was glad to put the city behind her now. The trip had been better than she could have hoped for, but she was ready for peace and quiet at home. She grunted a little, slightly irritated, as the crowd moved in unison to some unknown, subconscious rhythm, completely foreign to her, that kept them moving ever forward and ever onward.

With a quick thought, she made a sharp turn toward the bathrooms. She pushed open the door with her elbow and went in to relieve herself. In the stall, she hung her oversized, clunky backpack on the hook, fumbled with the buttons on her pants, and squatted over the toilet. Closing her eyes, she breathed a little sigh of relief. She paused and looked up, greeted by a cryptic message on the stall door, written in red lipstick in big, bold letters.

She still flies, this beautiful angel, even with her broken wing.

Juju stared at the words with a blank and tired face. She dabbed herself, stood up, and pulled up her underwear and pants. Just before she opened the stall door, she looked at the message again for a long moment.

She liked it. "Yep," she mumbled to herself, putting her backpack on, "I do like that beautiful angel motherfucker."

Before leaving the bathroom, she washed her hands and looked up at her reflection in the mirror. She looked good, she thought. Tired but good. She tilted her head from side to side, took one last glance at herself, and walked out.

Seconds later Juju was back in the throngs of the main concourse of Penn Station, working her way to the Amtrak platform. Her train was scheduled to board in twenty minutes. She sidestepped the crowd and made her way toward the wall full of Broadway play advertisements, ads for cell phones, and beautiful people wearing the latest fashions. She leaned her back against the wall, pulled the hood up over her head, and waited. She felt safe in her little cocoon with her arms wrapped tight around her breasts and the world visible only through the little, round porthole right in front of her.

She still flies, this beautiful angel, even with her broken wing.

That little scribble was now stuck in her head. Not knowing exactly why she liked it, she saw the powerful quote spinning around and around, as it danced and pirouetted in her head. She thought of herself and what her life had become, this little angel with a broken wing.

Still, she flies. Still, I fly. Still, I fly, she thought defiantly.

Something made her wonder whether someone with a broken heart had written it or maybe someone without a broken heart. Did it matter? Not to her. *Fuck it*, she thought as she pulled the drawstrings on her hoodie tighter. The little porthole she was seeing the world through closed just a little more. This made her feel better. It made her feel safer.

Lost in thought, Juju slowly slid down the wall, and as she landed on her ass, a little *umph* escaped under her breath, reminding her of the bruise she had gotten during her Columbus Circle adventure on Wednesday. She pulled her knees to her chest and pulled her beat-up backpack next to her. She waited patiently for the announcement that her train was pulling into the station.

CHAPTER 29

As Juju looked at the world from the floor of Penn Station, sitting beneath the latest Calvin Klein ad, Jimmy weaved his way through the swarm of people, all flocked around the big electric schedule board. He looked up to find his train back to Pittsburgh was on time, but the board didn't show the track number yet. He shot a quick look to his left and just barely noticed the little figure on the floor of the station. To his right, Jimmy was distracted by an Amish family nervously huddled together. The little Amish girls' eyes darted back and forth while she clung to her mother's plain gray dress.

Just then, the mechanical voice announced the boarding of The Pennsylvanian, Amtrak train 2112 to Pittsburgh on track nineteen. Jimmy silently bid New York farewell and followed the flow of travelers toward track nineteen. There were two lines to board the train: coach and business class. Jimmy had a business class ticket, so he cut through the crowd to the shorter line, ignoring the looks from the coach passengers.

Jimmy took a steely look around, and just then, he could see the back of her. The girl was sitting on the floor. She was just a wisp of a thing. Smaller than Jimmy by almost a foot. He looked from side to side to survey who was within earshot, then bent down and said to her, "You know, I always pay for the business class ticket, just so I don't have to wait in the long line. It's so worth it, isn't it?"

Juju looked up at Jimmy through the cozy porthole of her hooded sweatshirt. She smiled and said, "I agree. I do too." She turned back around and smiled to herself as the short line began to move and passengers began to board.

Jimmy's long legs walked past her quickly, and he started down the platform to the train. Juju raised her eyes from the ground to see him pass her. She switched her backpack to her other shoulder, looked back down, and followed him.

Jimmy thought how strange it was he had even spoken to her. It was incredibly out of character for him to do that.

He walked quickly down to the car, all the way to the back of the train. He nonchalantly turned his head as he was walking to see whether the girl in the hooded sweatshirt was behind him. Much to his surprise, she was. He liked this. Although he was quickly outpacing her, she was definitely following him. He grabbed the railing and swung himself up the stairs, and into the car.

A minute later Juju stepped onto the train and looked back at the gritty platform of Penn Station one last time. *Goodbye, New York*, she thought as she stepped inside.

She saw him almost immediately, the guy who had talked to her in line. He was settling into his seat toward the back of the car. They locked eyes for the briefest pause, and then she took two steps toward him. They locked eyes again, and she was stuck. She didn't want to move and didn't know why. She quickly pretended to look around for a seat.

"Do you want to sit here?" Jimmy asked with an almost sheepish childlike poise. It was as simple as that.

Juju smiled, and without saying a word, she tossed her backpack above the seat in the luggage bin and sat down.

CHAPTER 30

Juju pulled her hood back down, and he saw her face for the first time. Red hair, big blue eyes, her skin a little pale. She was almost elflike in a very strange yet beautiful and intriguing way. She had the face of a woman who might be just a little older than he would think. The kind of face people glance at twice, because they can't figure out what, if anything, they like so much about it.

They sat in the last set of seats at the back of the car. There were only about twenty people with them in business class, which was a rarity for a Friday morning. Most seemed to be businesspeople reading the morning paper and drinking coffee, oblivious to the world around them. The pair sat in solitude together, and for a moment, neither was sure of what to say.

At last, Jimmy turned toward her and said, "My name is Jimmy … Jimmy Andrews."

She smiled a grand smile and replied, "I'm Juju … Juju Apple.

They awkwardly shook hands and kept them clasped for just a brief second longer than normal. Anyone watching probably wouldn't have noticed such a small gesture, but both Juju and Jimmy did.

"We both have the same initials. J. A." she said, adjusting herself in her seat.

Jimmy smiled and nodded. "We sure do."

Her name reminded him of candy for obvious reasons. He liked it. It seemed to fit her look with the red hair and blue eyes. He was trying to remember whether he had read a book that had a character in it named Juju. He didn't think so; nevertheless, he liked it.

Juju turned her whole body to face him and asked, "Are you going to Pittsburgh or someplace else?"

Jimmy replied, "I'm going to Pittsburgh. Well, I live in Struthers, Ohio, but the train doesn't stop there anymore, so I catch the train in Pittsburgh."

"How far away is Struthers from Pittsburgh?" she asked.

Jimmy shrugged. "About an hour."

She nodded with light and airy interest.

"How about you? Pittsburgh or someplace else?" Jimmy asked.

She smiled and boasted. "I'm a Yinzer girl."

Jimmy gave a smiling grunt of approval. He knew there were two types of Pittsburgh girls: those who admitted they were Yinzers and those who wouldn't. Jimmy liked that she was the first of the two.

"How come the train doesn't stop in Struthers?" Juju said.

She was staring at him intently. Her face was just a little closer than a normal person would sit and talk, and he could literally taste her sweet peppermint breath. If it was anyone else, he would have been extremely uncomfortable with it, but with this stranger, this woman he had just met, it was desirable for some reason.

"I don't know why the train doesn't stop in Struthers anymore. I guess just not enough people. I have to catch the train in Pittsburgh, no big deal though," Jimmy said.

Just as Juju was getting ready to ask another question about Struthers, the train conductor started walking down the aisle toward their seats. They sat up straight with eyes at attention as the conductor approached. They looked at each other, holding back a giggle, struck by the conductor's hat, which they both silently decided looked, well, just plain silly.

"Howdy, folks," the conductor said as he checked their tickets.

"Hello. I like your cap," Juju said.

"Fuck," Jimmy said under his breath and quickly turned to look out the window. He was breathing deep to hold back his laughter.

"Well, thank you, young lady." The conductor moved on, tipping his cap.

They leaned into each other and laughed. "My God, do you think he knows how kooky that hat looks?" Juju said and continued, "The poor guy looks like a freakin' pin monkey in that hat! I'm calling Amtrak's fashion police department!"

They both laughed, looking at each other with bright, squinty eyes, their smiles shining through.

The train slowly started it's run out of Penn Station under the Hudson River and into New Jersey. Juju and Jimmy started the slow and cautious task of getting to know one another. It felt like a slow dance, with neither wanting to dance too close. Not yet. After some polite and oddly comfortable small talk about New York and various other niceties, what happened next seemed inevitable.

Just as the train came out from under the river, Juju asked Jimmy blankly, "Soooo … Do you have a chick? Are you married? Do you have kiddos?"

Jimmy gave a little sniff and looked at her. "No kids and no chick." He instantly felt like his mouth was full of loose rocks. He quickly assumed that when he told her about Kristy, she would never understand. She would never get it. Nobody got it.

Jimmy looked at her, then down at his feet and sighed. "My wife, Kristy …" He took a long pause. "She died in July. July third. So I guess that makes me a widower."

She slowly stood up in the aisle, looking down at Jimmy, slack jawed. She felt as if all the air had been sucked out of her lungs while Jimmy was looking down at his feet.

"Jimmy," Juju said in a harsh whisper as she tried to keep her balance on the rocking train. Her legs felt wobbly. She felt slightly faint. Jimmy looked up at her startled face. In that instant, those big blue eyes filled with tears.

"Did you say your wife died in July?" she choked out the words.

He nodded and looked out the window at the buildings leading into Newark, New Jersey. Juju sat back down with a thump and stared at the seat in front of her. Neither spoke for a minute; then Juju touched Jimmy's arm, and he looked at her.

Juju said, "Jimmy, my husband, Sidney—he died in July too. He died on July third."

It felt like a bolt of lightning out of the clear blue sky had stuck down on the seat between them, and their souls melted, puddled, and ponded onto, and into, each other.

After a minute Jimmy said, "Juju. I'm so sorry."

"I'm so sorry for you, too," Juju said matter-of-factly, her blue eyes still filled with tears. They sat still, not talking, each quietly crying as the train sped through the city of Newark. The horn blew in the background as the rails curved through the New Jersey landscape.

Juju was the first to speak in a choked voice. "Jimmy ..."

He looked at her. They sat there, looking at each other for a moment; then Juju dropped her eyes. She didn't know what the right words were to say.

Finally, Jimmy said, "This is such a strange coincidence, isn't it?"

She didn't answer.

Jimmy sighed with a hint of finality. "Was your husband's name Sid or Sidney? I mean, what did you call him?"

She smiled, used the back of her hand to wipe away the tears on her face, and said, "I called him Sidney most of the time."

"How did he die?" Jimmy asked softly.

Juju started to cry again. Her face was buried in her hands as she leaned forward. Jimmy put his hand gently on her shoulder. "I'm sorry. I shouldn't have asked. I'm sorry."

Juju looked up at him. "No, it's fine. Sidney died of pancreatic cancer. It's just ..." Her words spun out in an astonished chuckle. "Your wife died too, on July third, just like Sidney."

Jimmy replied, "She did. It was a shitty summer. Am I right?"

Juju laughed a little. "You got that right. A shitty summer, fall, and winter. How did she die?"

Jimmy drew a deep, stuttering breath. "She had a heart condition we didn't know about. It's called ARVD. She died instantly at home with me. In my arms. I'm glad for that."

Juju nodded in complete understanding. They both slowly absorbed the providence of this strangely divine moment.

The train slowly came to a stop at the Newark train station. They both looked out the window to watch the people from all walks of life board and depart the train. They both had a peculiar curiosity in people and their stories.

Juju sat back. She badly wanted to change the mood. "Why were you in New York Jimmy? I mean, what were you doing there?" she asked cautiously as if it was a loaded question.

"I'm a photographer, and I had this bridal shoot thingy in Brooklyn for a magazine," he said casually.

"Ohhh! So you're an artist of sorts?" She beamed at Jimmy, with her tears quickly drying up. She knew a few very good photographers, and she wondered whether Jimmy was any good.

"I am, of sorts, I guess. I do love art. What about you? What do you do? And why were you in the Big Apple, Juju Apple?"

"Well," she said without hiding her pride, "I am an artist, and I was working too."

She noticed that Jimmy looked perplexed at yet another coincidence that had landed in their communal laps. How strange their symmetry seemed.

"What type of photographer are you?" Juju asked with great interest.

Jimmy replied, "Well, I do mostly weddings and fine art photography. Yet weddings pay the bills. How about you? What type of artist are you?"

Juju was eyeing his box of Mrs. Fields cookies, which he had pulled out of his backpack. He held out the box and offered, "Train cookie?" while laughing and shaking the box in front of her. This struck Ju as ridiculously funny.

"Train cookies!" She laughed aloud. "Did you call them 'train' cookies?" she said, laughing.

Jimmy watched her whole face open up with that smile. "Well, do you want one?" he asked with a big grin.

"Of course I do!" Ju said as she grabbed the little box and emptied five of the tiny cookies into the palm of her hand. She looked at them closely, then popped them in her mouth one at a time. "Ugh, these are gross," she said as she continued to eat them despite her chippy review.

"So, what type of artist are you?" Jimmy asked her again.

"I'm a painter. You know, the kind that people hang on their walls," Juju said nonchalantly as she took a huge swig of water to wash down the chocolate chip cookies. "I sell my work to galleries and private homes, offices, and stuff. I was in New York to deliver a commissioned piece to this couple on the Upper East Side."

"Oh," Jimmy said, "you must be good."

"Well, I am. Aren't you?" Juju asked with feigned smugness.

"I suppose I am. I shoot a lot of elite weddings all over the world, so I guess I'm okay," Jimmy said, almost not believing it himself.

Juju nodded matter-of-factly as she handed Jimmy back his cookies. "Thank you. Hey, do you want to see my portfolio? I can pull it up on my laptop," Juju said.

He was instantly curious about what this strange and funny girl painted. And now he was even more curious about the girl herself. She stood up, pulled her laptop out of her bag in the luggage rack, and sat back down.

"The only thing that sucks about being a wedding photographer is that I have to commit to clients months, even years, in advance. That really sucks, but whatever," Jimmy said.

"Committing to a wedding is about the only thing I can commit to these days. The reality is, I can't commit to shit. I don't even buy green bananas," Jimmy confessed as Ju tried to get the Wi-Fi to work on her laptop.

She looked up at Jimmy and started to laugh. She had an amazingly unique laugh. It had a peculiar musical laugh, the kind that when people heard it, they looked around to see who it was. It was deep and genuine, and sounded just a little masculine yet in a feminine way.

"You're fucked up," Juju said, typing in her password to her portfolio port. "Okay, here you go," she said, dropping her laptop on his lap. "Here's some of my most amazing stuff."

He was struck immediately by Juju's use of color and texture. She seemed to favor bright and brilliant shades of reds and magentas. He found it all to be very cool and eye catching.

Jimmy said, "Juju, this is good shit! No wonder you are in such demand."

She beamed and blushed a little. He slowly scrolled down the pages of artwork she had created. One particular piece struck a chord. The painting was of two large hearts, one red and one blue. They were painted in almost cartoonish simplicity, and that simplicity appealed to him. Jimmy pointed at it. "Ju, I love this piece," he said as he looked at her. "It's wonderful."

"I'm glad you like it. I painted that when I was drunk on strawberry wine." She smiled, arching her eyebrow. "The original now hangs in a certain rock star's house, who shall remain nameless."

Jimmy was openly impressed with that nugget of information. "Wow. Are you serious? I'm impressed!"

Juju shot him a look of humble gratitude and reserved pride. "I am serious. And thank you."

"I wish I could draw," Jimmy said as he continued scrolling through her work. "I can barely do stick figures," he said, smiling.

Ju said, "I wish I had an eye for photography, but I just don't."

"Well, Ju, you sure have an eye for color and form. I am a fan of your work!" Jimmy said, closing her laptop and handing it back to her as he stood up. "I have to use the bathroom." Ju nodded and pulled her legs tight against the seat so he could get into the aisle.

As soon as Jimmy was out of sight down the aisle, she jumped up, quickly opened the side panel on her backpack, and grabbed Max. She took out her favorite pen and scribbled, "Max! His name is Jimmy!" She quickly put Max and the pen away and sat down.

A few minutes later, Juju saw Jimmy walking down the aisle, back toward her. Jimmy was looking at her, and she made no attempt to lower her eyes. And neither did he.

Jimmy scooted past her and sat back down. Juju looked past him out the window and nudged his arm. "Look." She pointed. "Amish."

He turned to look and watched the horse and buggy in the distance. As the train sped forward, the buggy dropped from sight.

"Interesting lifestyle, eh?" Jimmy said with a tinge of judgment. "I saw an Amish family waiting at Penn Station. The little girl looked scared to death—you know, surrounded by the horde of strangers. I wondered why the fuck they would be in New York City."

Juju didn't answer right away, then surmised, "That's a good question. I mean, I doubt they were on vacation, right?"

Jimmy offered, "Probably not. Yet they are good with money. Amish farmers get a break on property taxes, some agriculture clause in the tax code."

"Jelly?" Juju said as she chuckled over his knowledge of taxes. "You would do it too if you could."

Jimmy laughed as she read his mind. He asked, "Have you lived in Pittsburgh your entire life?"

Juju smirked. "I have. Same with my parents and my grandparents. Three generations of Yinzers."

Jimmy smiled at this.

"How about you? Always from Struthers?" she asked.

Jimmy smirked in a strange, mirrored image of her. "Yeah. Three generations, like you." He switched the topic quickly. "Do you always take the train to New York?"

"Well, if I'm in a hurry, I'll fly. Yet most of the time, I'll take the train. Honestly, I love it. I mean, listen …" They sat still and listened to the train rumbling and rocking; then the train horn blew, and the sound, like a wave, floated by their window. "I love that," she said.

Jimmy nodded. "I agree. Sure, a plane or car is faster, but I don't know … it's not as, well, romantic."

Juju was looking at him. She felt exactly the same way. Like Jimmy, it wasn't about the money; she preferred the train. The experience. Like him, she would stare out the window at the passing scenery and get lost in her thoughts and emotions. She too would get a quick look at a farmhouse or row house and wonder what was happening inside. She too wanted to know the story of the faceless people we couldn't see.

"I feel it's romantic too," Juju said, smiling in agreement. "There is just something sentimental about all this." She opened her palms and looked around. "I'm a cornball, Jimmy! I love it too."

They sat in silence for a moment, taking it all in. Then Jimmy said, "Thanks for sitting with me, Juju."

She smiled, blushed just a tiny bit, and said, "You're welcome, Jimmy from Struthers."

They both stared out the window at the endless rows of houses as they entered, then quickly left, the frame of the window. Juju shifted her eyes to look at Jimmy. She bit her lip and smiled ever so slightly.

CHAPTER 31

As the train made its way toward Philadelphia, the minutes ticked by into hours. The pair chatted away with airy curiosity, sharing stories and getting to know one another. For Jimmy and Juju, everything seemed relevant and important.

"So, when is your birthday?" Jimmy asked nonchalantly.

Juju laughed a little. "I was born on April Fools' Day."

"No shit? Really?" Jimmy asked, slightly amused. "I guess that doesn't surprise me."

"When is your birthday?" she asked, contemplating his remark.

"September sixteenth, so nothing special," Jimmy considered by comparison. "I always wondered if it sucked being born on Christmas. Do you think they get extra presents, or is it all rolled into one big to-do?"

Juju smiled at his thoughtful observation and said, "My brother's birthday is on December twenty-third, and he gets gypped every year, so I give him his birthday present on my mom's birthday in August, because you're right. I mean, Christmas is the big-dog holiday. Christmas babies get lost in the shuffle."

Jimmy thought about that for a moment and nodded, saying, "That is a very thoughtful thing to do for your brother, Juju."

Juju smiled as she stretched and cracked her knuckles, then asked, "Do you like Christmas? What about vacations? Any favorite places to go to get away from it all?"

Jimmy gave a small smile in response to Ju's knuckle cracking and her asking three questions in a row. He said, "I love Christmas. Granted, this Christmas sucked bad." He sighed and continued, "But yeah, normally Christmas is great—going house to house, visiting all the relatives. And as far as vacations go …" Jimmy smiled slightly, and Ju leaned in with interest. "Every year, Kristy and I went to the Outer Banks with her family for a vacation. It wasn't just being at the beach. It was the ride down there that was just as fun. You know? There was this fruit stand. I think it was called 'Powell's' or something like that. It's like an hour from the beach, so every time we got to it, we knew we were getting close. Kristy used to make me stop there, where she would buy fruit and candy. God, she loved the trip down there. She looked forward to it every year."

They sat in silence for a second, then Jimmy continued, "We would rent one of those huge beach houses. The ones with, like, ten bedrooms. The whole family would cook and sit out on the beach and just talk. We would all swim in the ocean, despite the chilliness. It was great. We would go in the fall when the rates were cheaper, and most of the people were gone. Still, plenty of tourist stuff to do, that's for sure, but most of the time we just bundled up a bit and sat on the beach. Every morning I would get up before sunrise to go take pictures at the pier. I would sit there in the cold sand and wait for the sun to show its color over the horizon. I would see Kristy walking down the beach to me. Although it was still dark, I could tell it was her, because of her walk. She would sit down, and we would watch the sunrise together. I miss that, you know?"

Juju knew. She definitely knew. Jimmy looked out the train window as The Pennsylvanian rolled into Philadelphia for the hour stop so the Amtrak crew could switch engines for the trip to Pittsburgh.

As Juju was silently lost in her thoughts, Jimmy remembered those nights with Kristy—making love to her while the big glass doors were open in their bedroom and the salty ocean air was blowing into the room. As he watched her while she was on top of him, her soft moans mixed with the sound of the waves crashing on the beach, and she moved her hips in slow, sweeping circles. As if in thanks for the natural beauty of the moment, she would turn her head to look out at the Atlantic Ocean, her profile sharp and beautiful in the dim light of night. Her dark hair danced on her back as it cascaded down like waves in the soft ocean breeze.

With her back arched, Jimmy watched her face in the moonlight as she orgasmed. Then they sat out on their balcony, looking up at the black sky, dotted with millions and millions of stars. It was always wonderful with her.

"You okay?" Juju asked with her eyebrows raised.

"Yeah. Yeah, I'm fine. How about we get off the train and stretch our legs?" he asked.

Juju nodded, and they jumped off the train and leaped up the stairs into the huge open area of the Thirtieth Street Train Station.

"Whoa! How cool," she said, gazing up at the seemingly endless ceiling.

"Yeah, kinda cool, eh?" he said, standing shoulder to shoulder with Juju, both looking up. They stood still as the hundreds of travelers quickly walked around them.

"Want an ice cream cone?" Jimmy asked.

Juju smiled at him, and without saying a word, they walked toward the Baskin-Robbins stand near the long bank of ticket windows. They ordered mint chocolate chip for Jimmy and double chocolate for Juju. Then they walked out the front door to have a look around.

"Have you ever been any farther than inside the station?" Jimmy asked.

"No, never," Juju said. "Usually I don't even get off the train. I remember when I used to smoke, I would step off for a cigarette, but that was about it."

Jimmy looked at her, amused yet surprised. "You used to smoke?"

She shot him a slick look. "Yeah, a million years ago. How about you? Did you ever smoke?"

Jimmy smiled. "Yeah, me too. A million years ago."

They stole glances at each other.

Jimmy said, "You just don't seem like the type of person who would smoke."

She shrugged carelessly. "I know. Now that I think about it, I quit before I met Sidney. He never smoked. He was so health conscious. And he still got cancer."

The pair slowly walked around to the far side of the station. It was a beautiful day in Philadelphia, and they both had their heads slightly tilted up, catching the sun. The buildings around the station gleamed in the spring sun. They sat down on a bench overlooking the Schuylkill River. They sat together in silence as they enjoyed the view and their ice cream cones.

"Do you remember the first time you realized you loved Kristy?" Juju asked as she licked her ice cream cone.

Jimmy laughed a little. "Yeah, I do."

Juju leaned forward a little, anticipating his story. "Tell me more," she said.

"Well, we were both asked to coach a Little League baseball team. Frankly, I don't remember why on earth they asked us. I think the guy who ran the league was a friend of Kristy's stepfather, Jim. I'm guessing they knew something we didn't and were hard up to find anyone to commit. It wasn't a hard job to coach the kids, but it was a job to coach the parents! Anyway ..." Jimmy licked his ice cream cone. "We agreed despite our reservations about the whole thing."

Juju adjusted herself on the bench as Jimmy continued. "So we had to go to this meeting of the parents, coaches, and sponsors. It was in this basement hall on the south side of Struthers. Some social club you rented out for stag parties and that kinda thing. It was packed with people. Not a single open chair, so we had to sit on the floor in the back. The steam heat was blasting, and it was incredibly hot and uncomfortable. I remember thinking people were going to pass out. It was so hot. After like twenty minutes of the crowd throwing around stupid ideas, this guy, who must have been drunk, stands up and starts talking."

Jimmy smiled, remembering the scene. "As soon as he stood up, Kristy looked at me like, *What the fuck is this guy going to say?* He could barely stand up straight! So he started going on and on about how the teams needed to be more like NASCAR, with patches and all that stuff.

So Kristy started to laugh. I mean, really laugh. I looked over at her, and well, I started to laugh. There we were, in the back of this hot, shitty hall, laughing our asses off like a couple of kids in the back of the class at school."

Jimmy went on, "So, now everyone turned around, looking at us, and we are practically hyperventilating from laughing so hard. So Kristy starts to get up, which she can barely do from laughing so hard, and I grabbed her arm and said, 'Where are you going?' She blurts out, 'I just peed my pants!' Well, everyone is just staring at us, with their mouths gaping open. Drunk NASCAR man is standing there with his hands on his hips, looking at us, pissed off he was interrupted. Kristy is stumbling out the door, and the place is dead quiet except for Kristy's screams of laughter from down the hall. After a few seconds, I stood up with tears still streaming down my cheeks. The room is dead quiet, and everyone is staring at me, and I just said, 'I'm sorry. My girlfriend needs the bathroom. Please carry on.'"

Juju smiled and asked, "So that's when you knew?"

Jimmy nodded, his brown eyes ever so lightly tearing up. "I knew right then and there. I knew I would love her. I knew I would marry her. I knew she would be with me forever." He tossed what was left of his ice cream cone into the river. "So much for fuckin' forever, right?"

Juju stood up and stretched on her tippy-toes. "That is a great story, Jimmy. Yeah, fuck forever."

Jimmy looked at Juju as he stood up and said, "Yeah, well, maybe forever fucks you."

Juju shook her head, smiling. "You're crazy. We better get back to the train, or we'll be walking back to Pittsburgh with the tax-free Amish."

Jimmy howled at her remark as they made their way back into the train station. Juju looked at Jimmy and asked, "So, did you end up coaching?"

Jimmy howled even louder. "Fuck no. They asked us never to come back." They both laughed, and the sound echoed in the high ceilings of the grand station.

CHAPTER 32

The loudspeaker announced the boarding of Amtrak 2112 to Pittsburgh, so Ju and Jimmy dashed down the stairs to the lower-level platform. They enjoyed this impromptu foot race to the train, laughing as they jumped onto their car. Jimmy's long legs won the race.

Just as they were making their way to their seats, Jimmy slightly ahead of her, Juju had the urge to jump on his back for a piggyback ride, but just before she did, she thought, *No, too soon. Not now.* She smiled to herself and bit her lip.

"So, if you don't mind me asking, how did you and Sid meet?" Jimmy asked as he settled into his seat and loosened the laces in his shoes, getting comfortable.

Juju smiled. "Well, we both just happened to be at Target in Robinson Township. He was in the candy aisle, buying goodies for Halloween. There he was, holding two bags of candy, clearly trying to decide which one to get. I noticed him standing there alone, so me being me, I walked over and pointed at the bag of Milky Way bars, and said, 'Milky Ways are my favorite.' He looked at me, surprised, and laughed."

Ju took a deep breath. Jimmy couldn't tell whether she was happy or sad to recount the memory. He kept quiet and waited to see whether she would continue.

Juju beamed and continued, "We started to chat, and the next thing you know, we're eating Milky Way bars right there in the store. The people who worked there probably thought we were half crazy. Or mystery shopper candy tasters!" Juju said, smiling, as she fiddled with her pink watch with oversized numbers. "We checked out at Target and walked over to this hippie coffee shop across the street, and we had about one hundred cappuccinos between us. We spent most of the day there, talking and getting to know each other. It didn't take us long to know how good it felt just being with each other. No, it all seems like a million years ago, you know? Kind of like watching an old home movie. You know what I mean?"

Jimmy nodded; he knew all too well.

Ju pushed on with her story. "Our first real date was dinner down at Station Square, where we ate and watched this jazz band play. I didn't want to tell him how much I hated jazz, but oddly enough, I got the feeling he could tell. After dinner, we walked along the river, and the city looked amazing. It was just a great night, and things just kind of went on from there."

Ju went on, "Some of those memories seem so hard to relive now." They both sighed in unison. "I do remember that when I got home from Target, I realized I had a pocket full of little Milky Way wrappers." Ju smiled. "I put them in a little box I had on my vanity. When Sid died, at his funeral I put them in his pocket in his casket. All of them, except one. I kept one."

"I love that, Ju. I love it. Do you know what was hard for me?" Jimmy asked, fiddling with his hands."

"What?" Ju asked with sad curiosity.

"When to stop wearing my wedding ring. I notice you don't have yours on, right?"

She nodded with just an ever-so-slight hint of remorse and guilt in her big blue eyes.

Jimmy continued, "I remember feeling so guilty when I put it in a drawer in my bedroom. I looked at it for a long time before I finally put it away. I kept thinking, *Would Kristy be mad?* I guess it's just one of those little things you have to deal with as a widower. I asked a friend of mine for her opinion, and she was very frank. She thought it all boiled down to if I felt I was still married. Am I? Are you?" Jimmy looked at her, waiting for an answer.

Juju didn't have an answer. She found it strangely comforting that they shared the same thoughts. Finally, she said, "I wore mine for a little while, but for me, it was this constant reminder that I *used* to be married. Every time I looked down, I would remember Sid, and that's not always a good thing. I know how horrible that sounds, but it's the truth. God forgive me, but in the beginning, there were times when I didn't want to remember him. I wanted to breathe again and take a break from being so fucking sad and crying so fucking much."

She took a deep, choppy breath and continued, "I woke up one night, and my ring finger hurt. Isn't that strange? My finger physically hurt. I sat up in bed and held my hand in front of my face with only the moonlight to see with. I took it off, Jimmy. I put the ring on my nightstand and laid back down. The next morning I put it in my jewelry box, and that's where it is now."

They both sat in silence for a moment. The train took a slight corner, and they both swayed with it. Juju looked at him out of the corner of her eye as he rubbed his ring finger. She wasn't sure whether he was crying.

"Jimmy ..." Ju swallowed hard. "Jimmy, sometimes I feel so fucking lost. Like a part of me is missing. Like a piece of my soul is gone. A void in my being. I always wonder if this feeling will ever go away. Everyone always tells me that time will heal my pain, that Sidney is watching over me, how I need to be strong, blah blah blah. Fuck that, and fuck all of them." Her voice raised in defiance as she spoke. Jimmy smiled sadly and looked out the window at the passing green scenery.

Juju raised her arms over her head and stretched. "Fuck it," she said, dismayed as the train horn blew its long and sad song, echoing from the front of the train.

"Do you have any siblings? Brothers? Sisters?" Jimmy asked, changing the subject.

"I have a brother, Matt. He's married and has two daughters, my nieces, Samantha and Marisa. His wife's name is Abby. They all live in Pittsburgh. I call my niece Samantha 'Sammy the Bull.' She hates it," Juju said with a smirk.

"What does he do for a living?" Jimmy asked out of curiosity.

Ju said, "He works for an insurance company. It's strange. That's the last job in the world you would think he would have. He's funny—always a good time, you know? I never thought he would be a suit-and-tie kinda guy, but he is."

"What does he do in insurance?" Jimmy asked.

Juju scrunched her face. "I'm not exactly sure. Something with life insurance. Matt was a big help when Sid died. We had life insurance on each other, and that was helpful. It let me pay off the house, the studio, all our bills. It was good to have that wiggle room." Juju was fidgeting just slightly, tapping the tips of her fingers on her leg.

Jimmy got the feeling that perhaps she was uncomfortable talking about the subject.

"I have to go pee," Juju said with a slight chuckle. Jimmy smiled and gestured for her to go.

CHAPTER 33

As soon as Juju got up to go to the bathroom, Jimmy took a deep breath and rubbed the back of his neck. He was nervous and afraid it might be showing. He was slightly dismayed by his lack of charm. It dawned on him that he hadn't needed to charm a girl in so many years. He honestly didn't know whether he *was* charming her or whether he should even be trying. She seemed to be so open with him, but was that just because of their situation, both being widows? He couldn't tell, not yet anyway.

Was it possible she liked him? He didn't know. Almost immediately he dismissed the thought. It had been so many years since these things had even crossed his mind. The word *crush* popped into his head, and that made him smile. Did he have a crush on this girl? His slight laugh was just barely audible as he brushed the thought away.

Juju came back from the bathroom and sat back down. "Do you want to play twenty questions?" she asked Jimmy with fun in her eyes.

"Well, I guess I do. Are you asking me the questions, or am I asking you?" Jimmy asked.

"I'll ask you," Juju said as she leaned toward Jimmy, giving him her best inquisitive look. "Okay, I'm gonna be tough on you. No silly softball questions here."

Jimmy smiled. "Give me your best shot."

Juju started. "What's your absolute favorite soda pop?"

Without skipping a beat, Jimmy said, "Grape Crush. Ever try it?"

Juju smiled grandly and said, "Fuck yes! I love Grape Crush! I can't believe you like Grape Crush. That is so fucking awesome. It's been my favorite since I was a kid." Juju smiled big with approval as they continued back and forth.

"Who was the first girl you kissed?"

"Jody Goldsmith."

"Secret celebrity crush?"

"Winona Ryder."

Juju cocked her eyebrow. "Vampire, werewolf, or mummy?"

"Vampire, of course."

Juju nodded in approval. "What's your dream job?"

"I have it. A photographer."

"Money or love?"

"Damn … okay, money, I guess. No, both."

Juju cracked up. "Have you ever shoplifted?"

"No, never, believe it or not," Jimmy said.

Juju confessed, "I once stole a candy bar from the corner store. I was twelve. I felt horrible, so the next time I went into the store, I stuffed a dollar into the box of chocolate bars, and I ran out!"

Jimmy chuckled at the thought of her at twelve.

Juju continued. "Sunrise or sunset?"

"Sunrise."

"Cake or pie?"

"Cake. Definitely cake."

"Silver or gold?"

"Silver. It seems more timeless to me."

"Favorite vintage candy?"

"Oh, easy. Skye Bar."

"Ferrari or Lamborghini?"

"Ferrari."

"Bigfoot or the Loch Ness Monster?"

Jimmy laughed at this. "Bigfoot, baby."

Juju suspected there might be a story there. "Baseball or football?"

"Baseball. Baseball. Baseball."

"Oatmeal or chocolate chip?"

"Chocolate chip," Jimmy said as he grabbed the now-empty Mrs. Fields chocolate chip box, shaking it in front of her, smiling.

"Jell-O or pudding?"

"Pudding for sure."

"Is that twenty questions?" Juju asked.

"Probably close enough," Jimmy said, chuckling.

"Who was your first kiss?" Jimmy asked. "You asked me, so now I get to ask you."

Juju nodded. "Fair enough. It's kinda boring, though. Teddy Emporellis. I was seventeen, believe it or not. A late bloomer and kind of a nerdy kid. I was all knees and elbows, as the saying goes. All I did was draw, read, and daydream. I didn't have any interest in boys until maybe sixteen. I think my parents thought I might be gay." She gave a slight chuckle. "Eventually, I came out of my shell. This boy, Teddy, asked me to the movies. He was in my advanced English lit class, and I knew he had kind of a crush on me. I remember sitting in the cafeteria, drawing sketches, and I would catch him stealing a glance. My folks were thrilled when he came to pick me up, and I remember he had an old pickup truck that was bright red, with a red vinyl interior. One look at that truck, and my parents weren't so sure. Teddy drove us to The Southside Works for dinner and a movie. I remember being very, very excited. After the movie, we drove up to Grandview Avenue and walked to one of the outlooks—you know, the ones that overlook the city? We were both nervous. He leaned over and kissed me. It was nice. There were no fireworks or anything like that. We had a few more dates, but soon enough we just kind of quit talking, and things just sort of fizzled out. I never told him that he was my first kiss. I never told anyone, until you."

Jimmy was listening intently. "Do you ever talk to him now?"

Juju shrugged indifferently. "I'm friends with him on Facebook, if that counts for anything. Teddy still lives in Pittsburgh. I know that. I think he's a car salesman over in Robinson Township. I think he sells Kias. Someone told me he was married a couple of times and has a couple of kids. I heard one of them got drunk and tried to climb the Roberto Clemente Bridge after a Pirates game. His kid got stuck up there, and the fire department had to come to get him down."

Jimmy looked at her, wide eyed. "Really?"

Juju laughed a little. "So, that's what I heard. I mean, think about it. How the fuck do you climb that bridge to the point where you can't get down?" she said, smiling.

Jimmy laughed. "You certainly know some interesting people."

Juju said, "Well, my circle of friends now is fairly normal, even in the art world. People assume if you run in those circles, everyone is somewhat eccentric. I have never really experienced it like that. Most of the people I know in the art world … I mean, look at what we do as a business—and not for some grand, flighty purpose. They are motivated by money, same as you and me. Am I wrong, or am I right?"

Jimmy thought for a moment and nodded. "You're right. I do what I do to make money first and foremost. If I can make an impact on someone with a photograph, then that's wonderful, and that makes me happy, but so does depositing their checks in the bank."

Just as Jimmy was making his point about money, Juju chimed in, "Jimmy, if you made no money from photography, would you still love it? Would you still do it?"

Jimmy looked thoughtfully out the window and replied, "Yes. Yes, Ju, I would. I just figured out who wanted to pay for it."

Juju smiled. "Yes. That's a dream come true."

CHAPTER 34

As the train rolled smoothly into the Harrisburg Station for a fifteen-minute stop, Juju leaned over Jimmy and looked out the window. "Do you want to jump off real quick?"

Jimmy said, "No, I'm okay, unless you do."

Ju seemed in a hurry and leaned forward to tie her shoes. "Hang on. You stay here. I'll be right back."

Juju scampered off the train in her funny way. Jimmy watched her run by the train window and disappear into the station. A few minutes later, Ju came bounding back, holding two vintage bottles of Grape Crush sodas.

As she ran back to the train door, she saw Jimmy looking out the window at her. She held the two sodas high above her head with a triumphant smile as she continued to the door. She ran down the aisle and sat back down, breathing heavily.

"Wow! Where did you get those?" Jimmy said, excited.

Juju beamed back. "There is this little store inside. I took a chance."

He looked at her, amazed. "I fucking love Grape Crush!"

"I know you do! Question one," she said with a cocky smile. She twisted the purple bottle cap off and took a swig. "Ahhhh. That's better than I remember."

"It's the bee's knees," Jimmy said, smiling, twisting off his cap.

Juju laughed. "The bee's knees? What the fuck is that?"

Jimmy was a little embarrassed. "It's one of those sayings from the 1950s. It means something wonderful, like the cat's meow."

"Oh, I see," Ju replied. "Here's to the Goobersmooch meow!" She giggled. "That's my amazing cat!"

They smiled at each other. Jimmy raised his bottle of Grape Crush, and Juju raised hers.

"A toast," Jimmy said. "Here's to everything wonderful in the world." He paused for a second. "Here's to us, Juju."

She smiled that big smile Jimmy already knew by heart and said, "Here's to us, Jimmy."

They drank their Grape Crush as the horn blew, and the train readied to leave Harrisburg, heading toward Pittsburgh. Toward home.

Jimmy and Juju laughed and talked like two long-lost lovers who had somehow found each other after so many years apart. Anyone who walked by them might have mistaken them for a newly married couple who were on their way to their honeymoon. They couldn't stop talking, with their hands waving in the air to make a point, while recounting stories of childhood and stories of their lost loves, Kristy and Sidney. They helped each other laugh and cry.

Juju sat for hours with her hips turned toward Jimmy, trying her best to absorb everything about him, their faces closer than they needed to be as they poured their truths out to each other. They shared things no other person on the planet knew, even the embarrassing things that until now they could barely bring themselves to admit. For the first time, they let themselves slip out of grief and into this new world, a world where, for now at least, sadness washed away and the sun finally came out. They were both able to open up and shed the layer of hurt, revealing new skin. For the first time, they could speak without fear of someone not understanding how they felt.

There was so much more going on between them. Something primal, something ancient. Yes, they shared a common bond. But it was more. It felt like they needed to touch each other as they spoke as if to somehow transfer what they were saying into the other through touch, where words didn't matter. It was a connection made by instinct alone. It was like two passing ships lost at sea. And in a dark ocean of grief, together they found the other side, like a rite of passage to find hidden treasure, still exuberantly alive in one and still exuberantly alive in the other, just buried beneath the rubble. And it was good. It felt so good.

The train continued to run down the endless tracks. And the conversation between these two souls continued on and on. They sat across from each other in the cafeteria car and ate a late lunch of pizza and spring water. They learned they were both vegetarians and both hated hummus. They loved the same 1980s movies. They loved the band Rush and had since they were teens. They both loved sweets and had an unhealthy obsession with ice cream, cherry soda, and chocolate cupcakes with vanilla icing. Jimmy learned Ju hated popcorn, and Ju learned Jimmy had never eaten a tomato. They both shared the same curved sense of humor. They laughed at the same things at the same time. They read many of the same books and shared a similar distrust for authority. They both had a gypsy spirit hiding deep within them, and they both loved creepy things like monsters and everything that went bump in the night.

CHAPTER 35

"You know, my friend Marc thinks I should move to New York," Jimmy said, stirring his tea slowly.

"So, what do you think?" Juju asked, stirring her tea too.

"I'm not sure, to be honest," Jimmy said. "I don't have any reason to stay in Struthers. Kristy is gone, and I stayed in Ohio because of her family. I doubt they would care if I moved at this point. I've always been good with money, so I don't need to work as much as I do."

Ju nodded and gave a small smile of approval that Jimmy was a saver. This was important to her. Like Jimmy, she wasn't the stereotypical starving artist. She made good money, and she had family money too.

"How seriously have you thought about moving?" Juju asked.

Jimmy shrugged. "Well, seriously enough that I think maybe in a year I might do it. The idea of living in New York appeals to me." He sipped his tea and continued, "I mean, why not move? Where I live now is kind of—I don't know, Ju. Too many ghosts around. It's like living in a haunted house sometimes. I can't go anywhere or do anything that doesn't remind me of her. Every time I turn a street corner or go to the market, something there reminds me of her."

Ju nodded. She knew exactly what he meant. A thought began to quickly grow in her mind. As they talked and sipped tea, she imagined the two of them living in New York City together. Walking around lower

Manhattan on Sunday mornings. Living in a big loft in Soho. Sitting on a park bench and holding hands in Central Park. Enjoying warm autumn evenings in the city.

"How about you?" Jimmy asked. "Would you ever leave Pittsburgh for the Big Apple?"

Juju snapped out of her fantasy and pounced on the chance to feel Jimmy out a little. "Oh, for sure. I guess I stay in Pittsburgh for my family, too. If you think about it, you can fly home in an hour from JFK. If anything ever went wrong in Pittsburgh, I could be home in no time. That being said, yes, I would move there if an opportunity presented itself."

Right away Ju cringed on the inside. Did it sound like she wanted to move to New York with him? Was she being too forward? What was he thinking?

Jimmy did a great job of hiding his happiness with her response. They looked at each other, and they both had just a hint of a smile on their lips.

They made their way back to their seats and sat quietly for the first time all day. Both were lost in their thoughts, Jimmy thinking of Ju, and Ju thinking about Jimmy. They both drifted off into a light sleep. Juju's head slowly tilted and fell onto his shoulder as they slept. They napped peacefully as the train rolled and twisted across the Pennsylvanian countryside, the soft horn from the engine floating back like a restless spirit.

CHAPTER 36

"I have a dog named Taffy," Jimmy said out of the blue as he stretched from the catnap. "She's a greyhound I rescued from a track in Florida. She's a great dog. She sure sleeps a lot."

Juju laughed lightly. "I mentioned my cat, Goobersmooch. Just a basic cat. Nothing special or out of the ordinary, yet he's the cat's meow to me."

Jimmy smiled. "I absolutely can't dance. I mean, I'm horrible at it," Jimmy confessed. "I have two left feet for sure."

Juju in turn confessed, "I'm kind of, sort of, a really, really bad driver." She glanced at Jimmy with those big blue eyes as Jimmy silently dismissed her worry. She continued, "Jimmy, I'm serious. I just never got good at it. One time I took a left turn onto the Boulevard of the Allies, and I clipped a city bus. I mean, I fucked up the bus and my car. The entire side of my car had this huge scrape on it. And the bus had a bike thingy on the front. And the bike got fucked up too. You know what the worst part was?"

Jimmy, holding back an urge to laugh, shook his head.

"The TV news showed up, and there was even a fucking news helicopter flying right above us, because it happened at rush hour and caused such a traffic jam. There were people taking pictures and running around, and there I was, crying, while the kid who owned the bike was yelling at me, and the TV cameraman was recording the whole thing."

Jimmy had his hand over his mouth, trying to hold back his laugh.

"Then that night I was on the six o'clock news, and of course, they only showed me for like three seconds, crying with snot coming out of my nose, and I screamed right into the camera, 'I didn't see the bus!' Then they cut away. You can find it on YouTube if you look."

Juju looked at Jimmy, and they both burst out laughing. And couldn't stop. Jimmy leaned in to give her a hug. "Ju, wow, just wow."

Juju put herself in his arms and said, "It was fuckin' horrible. Thank God my insurance paid the bill."

Jimmy smiled at her silver lining as she pulled out her lucky silver dollar from her back pocket. She started to roll the silver dollar across her fingers. Finally, after several failed attempts, the shiny coin rolled easily from finger to finger to finger. Juju looked at Jimmy with a triumphant grin. Jimmy was clearly impressed and said, "So you're better with silver dollars than cars?"

Juju laughed. She tucked the silver coin neatly back into her pocket and said, "All right, smarty pants. You tell me something humiliating that you've done!"

Jimmy sighed and smiled. "Okay, Ju. When I was in the seventh grade, I played basketball after school, an intramural sports thing. I wasn't that great, so I didn't get much playing time. Then one day the coach pointed at me, and I jumped up, thinking this was my chance. Full of grit, I sprinted onto the court. After a few plays, this kid, Ernie, passed me the ball, and I was off! Running like an Olympic star, lighter than air, dribbling that ball down the court, I could hear everyone cheering and screaming as I made a perfect layup shot. I pumped my fist to the crowd in victory, Kirk Gibson style."

Juju interrupted, "Wait. Who the fuck is Kirk Gibson?"

Jimmy laughed. "He was a 1980s baseball player known for his fist pump after making a home run."

Juju said, "Oh, okay, okay. Go on."

Jimmy continued, "As I looked into the stands, my hands raised in victory to bask in the cheers of my classmates, they were all laughing at me. It took me a few seconds to realize I had made that incredible layup into the wrong basket."

Juju giggled. "Oh my God, Jimmy, you didn't! 'Run, Forrest, run!'" And they both roared in laughter.

Juju stopped laughing after a moment, took a breath, and said, "You know what Sidney told me before he died? He said that sooner or later I would come out on the other side. I didn't understand what he meant. Now I think he meant that eventually, I would move on without him. Is that too simple? Is that too easy? I mean, fuck. I can't go on forever in utter despair, can I? Sometimes I get mad at myself. I have most of my life in front of me. I have years and years in front of me. Is it okay to want to move on? Is it okay to wonder about a new life? I want children. I want to be happy again."

Juju was crying. "I don't like being a widow. I'm too fuckin' young, Jimmy! You're too young! It's just not fucking fair that our lives were pulled out from underneath us like this. I want so badly to come out the other side and see what's waiting for me. Maybe it's some new grand thing. Maybe it's a new life that I can only dream about. Whatever it is, I want to know. I want to come out on the other side of this shitty thing and say to God, 'Fuck off. You didn't beat me!'"

Neither of them spoke for a long minute. Finally, Jimmy said, "When Kristy died, I remember walking down the steps to my basement. I had a box of her stuff in my hands. I was going through her things, and it was a very, very difficult time. I was raging with grief. Out of nowhere, and for whatever reason, I said to God, 'Fuck you, God.' It felt so good at that moment to have God to blame. I lashed out at a God that I largely ignore because I wanted to blame someone or something for her death and my suffering. I'm not a religious person, but then I felt bad about it. Later that night, I knelt at the foot of my bed and prayed like a child to this God that took my wife from me. I told God I was sorry for saying that. I asked him to forgive me. Maybe it's a natural part of being human. Maybe everyone wants to blame someone for things that make no sense."

Jimmy looked at Juju somberly. "I've never told anyone that."

Juju looked at Jimmy, her eyes full of understanding.

Jimmy went on. "I feel like I could have been a better husband. A better friend. You know?" He paused to collect his thoughts. "I feel like I live with so much regret now. I should have, I could have, I would have. Why didn't I dance with her more? I don't know. We were so happy, but I still feel like, had I known our time together would be cut short, I would have done so much more." He turned the cap off his bottled water and took a quick drink. "Regret is a terrible feeling to live with, don't you think?"

They both stared at the seats in front of them.

"Jimmy, maybe it's just us?" Juju said. "I don't know about you, but sometimes I see couples fighting and arguing, and I don't get it. Do they have any idea how lucky they are? I want to punch them in their stupid faces."

This statement made Jimmy smile.

Juju laughed. "Are we fucked up? Are we?" she asked seriously

"Maybe. Maybe we are," Jimmy answered.

They turned and looked at each other, grinning. "Fuck 'em," Juju said, holding up her water bottle.

"Fuck 'em," Jimmy said as they toasted to being fucked up.

CHAPTER 37

As the train came into Altoona, Pennsylvania, Juju said, "Oh, wow. How cool is that?" as they began the huge, sweeping turn around the famous Horseshoe Altoona Curve.

"Kinda neat, huh?" Jimmy said. "It was engineered to lessen the grade to the summit of the Allegheny Mountains."

"Look! You can see the front of the train!" Ju said, craning her neck over Jimmy to see better. "Whoa. It's beautiful, isn't it? When I was little," she said, sitting back down in her seat with a plop, "my dad would take us down to Station Square, and we would sit and watch the big trains go by. I remember my brother, Matt, would wear this train cap. You know, the ones that train engineers wear. I used to bug him to let me wear it, but he never would. So, one day my dad bought me my own engineers' hat. I was so happy. I wore that cap everywhere I went. Not just at Station Square but everywhere. I probably had that hat on most of my time as a kid. One day my dad took us down the tracks a little past Station Square where a train was stopped, and the crew let my brother and me climb into the train cab, and I got to blow the whistle. Or is it called the horn? Anyway, that was the highlight of my summer." Juju smiled, remembering her dad,

"My dad had one of those train sets in the basement. You know, the kind with all the little buildings and tiny little trees," Ju continued. "Then one time, my mom was cleaning the basement, and she accidentally spilled Pine-Sol all over one of the paper-mache mountains. My dad came home and had a fuckin' fit. My mom was trying not to laugh as my dad was gently trying to pick up the mountain, but it was soaked, and it fell apart in his hands. We were all standing there in a row, trying not to laugh." Ju smiled, remembering the stories.

Jimmy was listening intently. "Ju, how did your dad die? When did he die?"

Ju said with a sad smile, "He died when I was in high school. He had a heart attack at home. My dad was my hero. He always knew just what to say to me. He's the one who told me I should be an artist. He told me that the world was a beautiful place and that it should be my job not to let people forget it. I've always been sad that he never got to meet Sidney."

Jimmy asked, "So, how about your mom?"

Juju continued, "So when my grandparents died, my mom sold the fabricating company. She made a lot of money on the sale, I'm told. One time I asked her if her dad would be okay with her selling—you know, it's so final. She told me that's what my dad wanted her to do—to sell the company to take care of herself and me and my brother, Matt, without the burden of running the business. My grandfather too was a pragmatist. He wasn't emotionally attached to growing the business. Taking care of his family came first with him, and I think he knew in the long run it would be best for my mom to sell and take the money."

"It's nice to have a good example to follow, eh?" Jimmy said.

Juju smiled in agreement and continued, "My mom and dad were very much in love. I always remember them being affectionate with each other, like constantly. They were always holding hands and kissing. My mom never dated after my dad died. She never really told me why. Perhaps it's their generation? I'm not sure. So, when Sidney got sick and died, my mom was heartbroken. She adored Sidney, just like her family adored my dad."

Juju turned to Jimmy and asked, "How did your parents take it when Kristy died?"

Jimmy shrugged. "Not good. My dad especially. I remember him hugging me at the hospital. He kept telling me it would be okay. He still has a hard time talking about her, I think. Of course, my mom was heartbroken, too, in shock."

Juju nodded with such genuine understanding. "So, both your parents are still alive?"

Jimmy nodded. "They are. They were married for years and ended up getting a divorce as soon as my sister and I were out of high school. It was probably for the best. I think they just grew apart. I never asked questions, but I get the feeling neither one of them wanted the marriage to work. I guess it's their right."

Juju started laughing. "Hell, I thought it was my right I would be married forever! "Didn't you?"

Jimmy sighed and thought about it for a brief second. "Yes, I did." He was silently thinking about his parents and how their marriage had failed. Yet he had never heard his parents fight or argue. *You just never know what happens in the silence between two people.* Jimmy was beginning to realize that on this fated train ride.

CHAPTER 38

"I never realized how dirty America is until I rode Amtrak to New York," Juju said, staring over Jimmy out the window. "I mean, Jesus Christ, look at the fucking filth!" she said, speaking louder than she thought, which made Jimmy smile.

As Juju went on her short tirade about the garbage around the tracks, Jimmy couldn't help but agree with her. True, the tracks were littered with garbage, especially around the bigger cities like Trenton, Philadelphia, and Pittsburgh.

"I wonder who's in charge of keeping the area clean," Juju said, "I'm guessing the railroad, maybe?"

Jimmy watched the garbage piled up along the rails outside the window. Only to him, there was a certain odd beauty and elegance to the garbage. He was slightly surprised Juju didn't see it, too. As an artist, Jimmy tended to look at things like garbage and find ugly inspiration in it.

Juju sighed and sank into her seat. "Tell me something, Jimmy. If you could go back in time, knowing then what you know now, would you have married Kristy? Would you go through all the heartache and pain, the absolute suffering? Would you? Would you?"

Jimmy didn't need to think about it. He answered quickly and firmly. "Yes. Yes, Ju, I would. It's all worth it." He was getting teary eyed thinking about Kristy. Jimmy turned to her and said, "If I ask you the same question, you would say the same thing about Sidney, right?"

Juju, with a hint of a smile, nodded and softly said, "Yes." Her smile lingered for a brief second before it got lost in thought.

"Can I tell you something, Jimmy?" Juju said.

He got curious because the tone of her voice was different, with a slight brush of shame in it. He barely noticed it, but it was there. It was enough to make him look up from his hands and look her in the eye. "Of course you can, Ju. What is it?"

"I had sex with this guy." Juju started to cry a little. "I don't know why I did it." She looked up at the ceiling as a single tear slowly rolled down her cheek. "The strange thing is, I knew I would regret it before I even did it."

Jimmy sighed deeply and looked at her. "Ju, it's okay. No one has walked in your shoes. In *our* shoes."

Juju laughed a little. "You're the only one that knows, Jimmy. Well, you and the guy I had sex with."

"How long after everything happened with Sidney?" Jimmy asked, hoping he wasn't overstepping his bounds and being intrusive.

Ju said, "December. So about five months, I guess, give or take. I was just so, well, lonely. I thought someone touching my body again would be, well, comforting. It wasn't. It was awful," she said, fiddling with her shoelace.

His heart sank for her, and he said, "Ju, I wish I was the one there for you at that moment. You are an angel, Juju. Maybe we are all born broken, and maybe that night you were an angel for him."

Juju beamed at how Jimmy healed her sorrow in an instant. She thought about the little poem written on the stall door in the bathroom at Penn Station.

She still flies, this beautiful angel, even with her broken wing.

Ju so wanted to tell Jimmy about the poem, but she didn't. She felt ashamed just one minute before, but now, after Jimmy said that, she wasn't. She smiled a grand smile at Jimmy, deciding he was her angel too.

They both sat in silence for a minute; then Jimmy finally spoke. "So, was it weird fucking someone new?"

Ju laughed and covered her face with both hands. "Yes! It was kinda horrible!" she said, laughing.

They both started to laugh as Ju leaned into him. She did truly wish she had waited, and maybe Jimmy would be her first. Juju tried her best not to let the obvious emotion show. She was overwhelmed with how close his thoughts were to hers.

Juju looked at Jimmy and said, "I have to run to the potty."

He smiled. "Do you need help?"

Juju rolled her eyes, "Oh yes. Yes, I do! With so many things!" She got up and scuttled to the front of the train to the bathrooms. The little amber light was on, indicating the bathroom was occupied. "Shit." Juju nonchalantly looked back over her shoulder to see whether Jimmy was watching her.

He wasn't. He was looking down at his phone.

Juju quickly stepped through the pass door into the next car. In a sudden sprint, she dashed through the cars; as every head turned to watch her, she made it to the cafeteria car. She jumped into one of the booths, pulled out her cell phone, and quickly dialed. She was all smiles.

Juju's mom and best friend, Cookie, was enjoying the sunny spring afternoon, planting her garden at her house in the Squirrel Hill borough of Pittsburgh. Arthritis was catching up with her, which became more noticeable while tending to the plants, and she thought maybe Ju would help her with the gardening this year.

Just then, Cookie's cell phone rang and startled her. She looked down at the screen, saw, "Ju," and quickly answered, "Hi, baby. I was just thinking about you. Are you still in New York. or are you home?"

Juju answered her mom excitedly, "Hi, Mom. No no, I'm on the train home. Mom, guess what?"

"What, Ju? What's up?" Cookie asked.

"Mom, I met a guy on the train." Ju bit her lip and held back a giggle as she talked. "His name is Jimmy, and he lives in Struthers, Ohio. He's a photographer, and he's really cute, and he's funny, and he's kind, and he makes me laugh, and Mom … Mom … his wife died the very same day as Sidney. Mom, he lost his spouse, just like me." Juju looked over her shoulder to see whether anyone was listening or watching. No one was.

Cookie's heart warmed while hearing her daughter's jubilant voice talking about this stranger. Then her motherly instinct kicked in. "Ju, are you sure he's … you know … not some kind of weirdo?"

Juju said, "Mom no, he's so great."

Cookie smiled. She felt a little gush of relief. She knew Juju; if she said he was fine, then he was. Her daughter had this precise sixth sense when it came to judging a person's character. Juju's grandmother Rose had the same ability. "Okay, Juju, tell me more."

Juju was speaking just a little louder than a whisper. The cafeteria car had some people in it, waiting for food and mingling around, and she didn't want anyone to hear her conversation.

"Mom, he's so great. We've been talking the entire trip. We ate ice cream, and we cried, and we laughed, and Mom, he's great, and I think he thinks I'm great, too!" Ju was talking very fast. She was excited, and this, of course, made Cookie smile too.

"Oh, Ju. He sounds wonderful," Cookie said joyfully.

Ju continued, "I know, I know. Mom, can you believe he's a widower? How strange is that? He talked to me at Penn Station while we were in line for the train. Then we ended up sitting next to each other on the train, and we just hit it off, Mom. He's funny, too. Did I mention that, Mom? He loves the beach, he has a dog named Taffy, and he loves Grape Crush! *Mom, he loves Grape Crush!*" Juju said a little louder and started to giggle.

Cookie got tears in her eyes as she listened to Juju go on about this new man on the train, Jimmy. She was happy to see her daughter so excited about something. She'd thought that after Sidney, maybe Juju was afraid to love again. Understanding Juju better than anyone, Cookie knew Ju had such a deep soul. Her exterior was so much fun and sometimes silly, but underneath was a spirit of deep longing and kindness.

"Mom, I have to go. I want to get back to Jimmy so he doesn't worry. Mom, he's great. He's really great. I just couldn't wait to tell you."

"Okay, Juju," Cookie said, "I love you. Be careful and call me when you get home."

Ju smiled. "I love you too, Mom."

Juju stuffed her phone into her pocket and spun around to get back to her seat. She moved quickly through the cars, scooting her way back to business class. She stopped at the bathroom, which was still occupied. No matter; she had just been so excited to tell her mom about Jimmy. So Juju took a deep breath, composed herself, walked confidently back to their seats, and slid in.

"Everything okay?" Jimmy asked.

"Yep. Everything is perfect," Juju said, smiling.

The train rumbled on through small towns and cities. The endless cascade of Americana dripped by and flung itself from the train's steel wheels onto the window. Jimmy and Juju continued their uninterrupted flow of conversation. It was perhaps the first time Jimmy had opened up to anyone since Kristy died. Maybe even more so. It felt so good. So strange and yet so good.

He imagined so many years later when he was an old frail man living in New York; he would sit on his favorite bench overlooking the mighty Manhattan Bridge and remember this day with great happiness and nostalgia. His cracked and wrinkled face would show a secret smile as he thought of the girl with big blue eyes and red hair he had met on that train that day. Oh, so many years ago …

CHAPTER 39

"Jimmy, where's the one place you want to go? No limits," Juju asked him as she tried to unwrap the chocolate muffin she had just gotten in the cafeteria car. "They fucking wrap these things so tight!" she said grudgingly.

Jimmy took it from her hands, slowly pulled the plastic wrap apart, and gave it back to her, smiling. Ju smiled back, thinking, *Yes, my hero.*

"Okay, so where do you want to go?" Ju asked again, picking at her chocolate muffin.

Jimmy cocked his head as if in deep thought. "London might be cool."

Juju took a bite out of her muffin and said with her mouth full, "I've been there." Only to Jimmy, it sounded like "Iifbuntherree."

"Don't talk with your mouth full," Jimmy jabbed at her, smiling.

Juju swallowed and wiped bits of chocolate from her mouth. "I said I've been there many times."

He arched his eyebrow approvingly.

"Where else do you want to go?" Juju asked again. "Tell me someplace you daydream about, not some tourist bullshit like London." She nudged him on.

"You know, Ju, there is this place I've read about." Jimmy positioned himself so he was face-to-face with her, leaning in so they were only a foot apart. "It's on the Washington state coast. It's called Ruby Beach. I guess it's covered with driftwood and has these huge rock formations on the beach. It sounds so beautiful. I think I want to go there someday. I want to sit on the beach at sunset and watch the fire in the sky. I want to sit on the sand and look at the fishing boats. Maybe collect some driftwood, and when the sun finally goes down, maybe I'll go out to one of those restaurants and sit close to the sand, have a nice glass of wine, and listen to the waves crash on the beach.

"Oh, Jimmy. That sounds so beautiful." Juju watched him intently as he spoke.

Juju could picture Jimmy sitting there, the sun setting on his face and the ocean breeze blowing as he closed his eyes and leaned in to kiss her. Ju smiled at Jimmy as she watched the fantasy in her mind and licked the chocolate muffin off her fingers.

"I'll get there someday," Jimmy said as he leaned back into his seat.

"I'm sure you will, Jimmy," Ju said. "I'm sure you will."

Train 2112, The Pennsylvanian, took its last, lumbering turn into Pittsburgh and cruised slowly through the Strip District neighborhood. It pulled into the Pittsburgh station, the crossing gates flashing and the horn giving one final, quick blast as the train hissed and stopped. Jimmy and Juju looked at each other, sadly smiling, knowing their trip was over.

It instantly dawned on Jimmy to ask her how she was getting home from the train station, so he asked, "Do you have a ride home?"

She laughed, saying, "No, I was going to get a Uber. Or can you take me home?"

Jimmy just nodded and smiled.

They gathered their belongings and stepped off the train. They looked around the platform, almost deliberately trying to stall for what little time they had left with each other. The sun would set soon, and Pittsburgh's spring air was thick and rich under the covered train platform.

Jimmy said with some finality, "I guess we're home."

Juju said flatly, "I guess we are."

They looked at each other, gave a pensive smile, and started to walk down the long platform. As they walked, their hands brushed, and they grabbed on to one another. They held hands for the first time. Juju bit her lip and smiled, and her heart fluttered like butterflies. At that moment, she wanted so badly to jump into Jimmy's arms, squeeze him, and never let him go.

Two strangers who had met just this morning were walking hand in hand down the train platform to a new life story yet to be written. Neither wanted this lovely day to end; they walked slower than the rest of the passengers, who quickly walked around them. They rode the escalator down and stepped off into the lobby, where the ticketing area was deserted, and only half the lights were on. Juju let go of Jimmy's hand to duck into the bathroom before the ride home, and as soon as she was out of sight, she took out a napkin she had gotten from the cafeteria car on the train and pulled her favorite pen out of her backpack. After a quick minute of thought, she neatly wrote, "She still flies, this beautiful angel, even with her broken wing."

She folded the napkin carefully and put it in her front pocket. She checked her face in the cracked mirror, washed her hands with the cold liquid soap, reached into her backpack, and pulled out her toothbrush. She brushed her teeth quickly, and, taking a deep and slow breath, she slowly walked back out to Jimmy.

He stood by the front door of the station and watched her walk toward him. He smiled, and she smiled back. He was attracted to her in a way he had never experienced before. He wondered just then, and not for the first time that day, what she might be like as a lover. How her breath might feel against his neck. How the slow curve of her hips might feel in the darkest of hours just before the sun came up. How she would taste on his tongue ...

"All good?" Jimmy asked, shaking off the reverie.

"All good," Juju said. She laughed to herself, thinking, *As soon as I get home, I'm gonna have to pee!* They walked out the front door of the station.

The garage was across from the train station. As they got to the elevator, Juju said with a wink, "Do you remember what level you parked on?"

Jimmy smiled and replied, "I don't remember numbers. I remember names. For instance, four is Lou Gehrig's number. So, since I parked the car on level four, I just remember Lou Gehrig. I know it's a strange system, but it's how I work."

This little quirk of his made Juju smile. She shook her head and thought how cute he was.

They stepped into the elevator along with three other people. They were all going to level four, Lou Gehrig's floor. Jimmy and Juju stared at each other during the entire ride. Their eyes never dropped from each other. It was as if they were looking into each other's souls. Juju and Jimmy got off the elevator behind the other people and walked through the garage to Jimmy's car. They loaded their bags into the hatch, and Jimmy opened the passenger door for Ju and took her hand as she slid in. Jimmy got in on his side and said, "You'll have to give me directions when we get to Mount Washington. I don't know that area well."

They drove in silence for a bit as they made their way to Juju's house on Mount Washington. Finally, Ju said, "Jimmy, I had such a great time with you. I know it sounds stupid, but this was the best day I've had in a very, very long time. Like forever. I mean it, Jimmy."

Jimmy smiled. "Yeah, for me too, Ju. So maybe we won't fuck forever?"

Juju smiled that smile.

Jimmy continued, "You know it is not like me, yet I am so glad I talked to you at Penn Station. I truly, truly am."

Ju smiled at Jimmy and turned to look out the window. As they passed the corner of Penn and Sixth Street, Juju noticed an older couple walking and holding hands. Ju imagined they were very much in love. She smiled at Jimmy and reached for his hand again. Jimmy took her hand in his and softly squeezed it.

As they started to cross Smithfield Bridge, Juju said quietly, "When I was a little girl, I thought this bridge was a castle." She looked up at the big, blue bridge as they passed it. "I thought someday I would live in it." She sighed. "Silly, right?"

"No. Not silly," Jimmy said. "I always thought it was weird that when you got older, you still wished for the same things. Maybe a different form yet still the same dream. I bet even now you wish you could live in a blue castle on the bridge."

Juju didn't answer. She didn't have to; he was right.

Jimmy turned left on Carson Street, then made a right on Sycamore and took the back way up to Mount Washington. Juju watched the cityscape of downtown Pittsburgh go by and said to Jimmy, "I love New York, but this view just never gets old."

Jimmy pulled into Juju's driveway, put the car in park, and turned off the ignition. Ju was fidgeting a little, knowing she didn't want to get out of his car. She wanted to be back on the train with him. She wanted to go to New York City with him. She wanted to kiss him. Jimmy was thinking the same thing.

Reluctantly they opened the doors at the same time, stepped out, and looked across the car roof at each other.

"You got everything?" Jimmy asked as he pulled her backpack out of the hatch.

She nodded, almost trying to avoid eye contact with him.

"Guess this is it," Jimmy said, smiling at her.

"I guess it is," Juju said, glancing down at her red shoes.

"Thank you, Juju," Jimmy said, trying and failing to hold back his tears.

Juju welled up, and they fell forward into each other's arms and held one another tightly. He could smell her hair. It reminded him of cherry bubble gum. The seconds spun out until they took a half step back and looked at each other. They were both crying very hard without any shame. Jimmy gently touched her cheek with the tips of his fingers, and she shut her eyes.

"Juju, I feel like my life is going to be better because I met you. You've shown me that I'm not alone. You make me want to be a better man. That is what an angel does," Jimmy whispered.

Juju took a deep breath and opened her eyes, looking up at him with awe. She reached into her pocket and put something in his hand. Jimmy looked down at the neatly folded napkin.

"Don't read this now. Read it later, okay? When you get home, read it when you get home, Jimmy. Promise me," Juju said.

Jimmy nodded, his head tilted as he looked down at the napkin and said, "Okay, Juju."

He walked back to the driver's door and opened it slowly. Juju stared at him, not wanting to move. As Jimmy climbed in the car, he turned to Juju and said, "Hey, Ju, remember that beach? Ruby Beach in Washington State? The one I was telling you about?"

Juju nodded.

Jimmy said, "Maybe soon, late summer—say, September first? Remember the date, Ju. Promise me you'll remember the date."

Ju nodded, understanding what he was saying to her.

"Maybe I'll see you in September?" Jimmy said with a smile.

Juju nodded again, unable to speak.

Jimmy got in his car and slowly drove off.

Juju stood at the end of her driveway and watched until his car dipped below the top of the hill, and he was gone. She stood there in her driveway for a minute, hoping he would turn around and come back. She suddenly felt a ping of longing for not being next to him.

Finally, after a long minute or two, Ju sat down on her front stoop and pulled her hood up over her head, sighing. She looked up at the soft, late afternoon sky, shut her eyes, and smiled. This was the first time her *heart* had smiled since Sidney died, and she quickly realized she was happy.

Juju sat with her elbows on her knees thinking about Jimmy and the wonderful day. "Maybe this is the bridge to the other side. Is this what Sid was talking about?"

Juju got up, swung the screen door open, quickly unlocked the door, and pushed her backpack and herself into the house. "Goobersmooch!" she bellowed as she ran into her office to her computer. Impatiently, she waited for the machine to boot up. When it finally did, she googled

Ruby Beach in Washington state and started to scan the beautiful images of the ocean and the driftwood, just like she had imagined in her mind while listening to Jimmy.

After a few minutes, she stood up and went to her huge map on the wall, which showed every place she had visited during her nomadic travels. She looked closely at the northwest USA and found Ruby Beach. From the shelf below, she pulled out a pin and Post-it note, and wrote, "September 1st Jimmy," and pinned it to Ruby Beach. She stepped back and took a long look at the map, which was dotted with hundreds of pins.

With a crooked, little smile, she went to the laundry room, opened her backpack, and pulled Max out. She went into her living room and sat crossed-legged on her comfortable couch. Goobersmooch jumped into her lap, purring. After a moment of thought, Juju bit her lip, smiled, and began to write.

Dear Max. Guess what??!!!!

CHAPTER 40

Jimmy slowly drove away with both hands tight on the wheel, watching Ju standing at the end of her driveway from the rearview mirror. He crested the top of the hill, and she disappeared. At the first stop sign, he thought about turning his car around and going back, but he knew he couldn't. Or shouldn't. He wasn't exactly sure why he felt that way, but the mind moves so quickly sometimes, and sometimes those gears can twist and bind.

Two blocks later, he pulled up to another stop sign and dropped his forehead on the steering wheel. *What just happened?* It was like someone had just thrown the proverbial wrench into his new, well-oiled, emotional machine. The same emotional machine he had been carefully rebuilding from scratch, like an old watchmaker at his beloved workbench. A small smile began to grow in Jimmy's tired eyes. He spoke her name in his mind. Juju Apple. That girl. Oh, *that* girl.

A car behind him beeped twice, and Jimmy looked up, startled. He quickly turned right onto Route 19 and joined the flow of heavy traffic north toward the airport, then on to Struthers and home.

He waited to read the note she had given him until he got home, as he had promised. So many times on the hour drive home, he wanted to pull over and see what she had written on that napkin. He stubbornly refused to give in to his urges. He wanted to keep his promise, so he waited.

An hour after leaving Juju's house, he pulled into his driveway and shut the car off. With his bags in one hand, he unlocked the front door with the other. He went into the kitchen and poured himself an oversized glass of orange juice and jumped on the counter. The house was quiet and still, with the last remnants of the setting spring sun painting the kitchen in streaks of orange and yellow.

Jimmy pulled the napkin out of his pocket and very carefully unfolded it. The words of the message stood out in stark contrast on the white paper napkin.

Written in Juju's artistic handwriting, Jimmy saw …

She still flies, this beautiful angel, even with her broken wing.

Jimmy stared at the message with his eyebrows raised just slightly. He knew exactly what it meant. That just maybe Juju could love again. Jimmy held the note to his heart. Finally, he drew a long, deep breath and jumped down from the counter, walked into his office, and sat down at his big oak desk. He opened the top drawer, gently placed the napkin inside, and closed it softly.

He let his eyes find the photo of Kristy on the corner of his desk. He stared at it with just a wisp of a smile on his face. It was a photo of Kristy sitting in a field of yellow tulips, holding her camera. She was wearing one of his flannel shirts, and her hair was tossed to one side, cascading down her shoulder. She wore her unmistakable smile on her face. Jimmy looked at the framed photo and finally picked it up, leaning back in his chair. He didn't cry; instead, he smiled and slowly traced the edge of the picture frame with his finger.

He finally spoke to her in a husky whisper. "Baby. I need you to tell me this is okay." Jimmy held the picture with both hands against his heart.

His eyes closed tightly. "Tell me this is okay. Tell me I can do this. Tell me this is okay. I will never, ever forget you. Please tell me this is okay."

After a long moment, Jimmy stood up and slowly went to the window, which overlooked the backyard woods. With Kristy's picture still in his hand and hanging down at his side, he stared out into the darkening woods. The fireflies were just starting to flicker and dance in the yard. The tops of the pine trees blew gently in the evening wind. Like the pines, his thoughts swirled as he thought of the girl he had promised he would love forever and the girl who had taught him what forever really meant. He stood by the window for a long time, waiting like a child to hear Kristy's soft voice tell him everything was going to be okay. Finally, with a deep and thoughtful sigh, he put Kristy's photo back on his desk, pulled his phone out of his back pocket, scrolled through to his newest contact, Juju, and began to type. "Hey, Ju. It's me. I made it home in one piece."

EPILOGUE

SEPTEMBER

They sat on Ruby Beach surrounded by the beautiful sea stacks and driftwood Jimmy had painted in her mind on the train. It was all so breathtaking and surreal. Juju and Jimmy, both clad in oversized sweatshirts and short pants with bare feet in the sand, sat together on the shore. The tourists had fled back to their suburban homes and jobs, leaving the beach deserted. It was quiet except for the wind and the crashing waves. The moon was full, just now appearing over the horizon in the western sky.

Juju was wearing the same sweatshirt she'd had on in the spring when they first met at Penn Station in New York City. Her hood pulled loosely over her head, like a frame around her face, the ends of her red hair dancing softly on her neck in the steady ocean breeze. The salty ocean air blew across their tanned faces, while brilliant hyper colors of red, orange, and purple painted the evening sky, like one of Juju's works of art. They sat close, hips touching. Jimmy could smell the soft fragrance of Ju's hair mixed with the salty sea air. Everything was wonderful.

They watched a small fishing boat bobbing in the ocean, silhouetted black against the colorful sky. Juju thought, *This is it. This is the bridge, and we are on the other side. Thank you, God. Thank you. Love never leaves. It just... changes.* Juju looked up at Jimmy with a content smile.

Jimmy looked into her eyes and asked her in a whisper, "Ju, do you think you can ever love again?"

Juju said simply, "Yes." Her head dropped onto Jimmy's shoulder as she whispered into his ear, "Yes. *This* is the other side. Angel mine."

CPSIA information can be obtained
at www.ICGtesting.com
Printed in the USA
BVHW080859120721
611731BV00001B/102

9 781665 708258